Critical Acclaim for Elizabeth Watasin

The Dark Victorian: BONES

"Read if you:
Delight in a heady, deeply satisfying blend of Victorian, Gothic and Romantic impulses.
Enjoy supernatural horrors subservient to true terror: Humanities Inhumanity.
Can drown lovingly in narrative that is equal parts prose and verse.
Like your steampunk whodunit with layers of delicious conspiracy and malicious intent."
—Worth Reading?

"Ms. Watasin's hasn't let down on the excitement of the plot or the rich tapestry of her world where the cold mechanical technology of Victorian England meets the glow of eldritch light. Pick this one up and give yourself a present... and here's hoping that book 3 will be out soon."
—My Ethereality

The Dark Victorian: RISEN

"There is a finely honed edge to *The Dark Victorian: RISEN*. Ms. Watasin's wit and imagination shine through the world of dark shadows and eldritch power and one quickly finds a home within the pages of this story."
—The Gilded Monocle

"I have no problem recommending this one, especially to fans of steampunk and other Victorian-era genres. I look forward to the next book in the series!"
—The Towering Pile

More books by Elizabeth Watasin

The Dark Victorian: Risen
The Dark Victorian: Bones

Charm School Graphique Vol 1

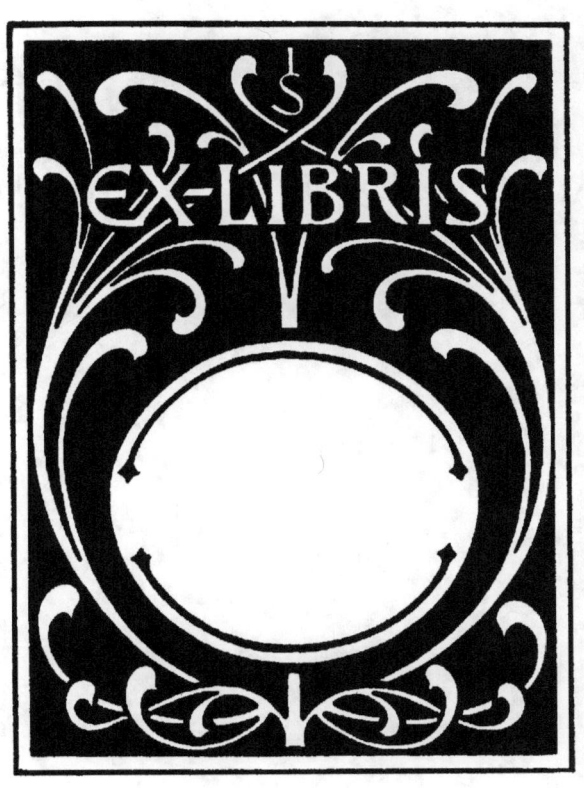

SUNDARK

An Elle Black Penny Dread

By
Elizabeth Watasin

A-GIRL STUDIO

An A-Girl Studio book
published 2013 in the USA.

For additional information, please contact:
A-Girl Studio
P.O. Box 213, Burbank, CA 91503 U.S.A.
www.a-girlstudio.com

ISBN: 978-1-936622-05-4
Library of Congress Control Number:
2013917029
First paperback edition, 2013

❖

Cover Illustration by Dara England
http://mycoverart.com
Cover Design by Elizabeth Watasin
Editing by JoSelle Vanderhooft
www.joselle-vanderhooft.com
Vintage spot illustrations from Dover Pictura

Hail
Hail
Hail
Hekate

CHAPTER ONE

On a humble street of Camden Town, amongst the tiny cottages of worker families and their green vegetable gardens, a small row of red-brick villas sat, facing one of the few paved streets. They were modest in size, only two stories, and edged with low iron fences protecting strips of trim flower bushes. Pensioners and lowly clerks might be found dwelling within. In the small walled gardens in back, herbs, fruit, and vegetables thrived from the recent spring rain, wet laundry swayed in the breeze, and on one plot a chicken coop stood, belonging to retired Royal Navy Lieutenant Elmer Montague.

Next to Lt Montague's home and in the middle of the row, a villa's entryway could be distinguished from the rest by the presence of a marble sphinx, her hair in curls and a shawl sculpted over her shoulders and leonine back. She smiled with her great paws laid out before her and didn't seem to mind that the top of her bosom peeked above her lace-trimmed bodice. Behind her, the red front door shone in the afternoon sunlight, and its polished black iron doorknocker gleamed.

Mrs Haggins, an older woman with silvered hair, walked down the sidewalk and turned for the gate leading to the red door. She carried a basket filled with sundries: soap for the dishes and laundry, a bottle of aspirin, a tin of black pepper, a paper bag of peppermints, a ball of white string, a sponge, a box of matches, and a copy of the magazine *An Englishwoman's Friend*. The date on the cover read: Monday, 15th March, year 1880. She opened the door and laid the magazine on the foyer's console table. She removed her bonnet and shawl and passed the parlour entrance for the kitchen, where she retrieved an apron and disappeared within.

The parlour was bright with sunlight that shone on the red throw rugs and stuffed chairs. A low fire in the fireplace crackled and warmed the room and several framed daguerreotypes and tintypes dotted the mantle. One tintype showed a man in a pith helmet, sitting astride a camel before an Egyptian pyramid. In the family portrait by the tintype, the same man stood with a woman, a dark-haired girl, and smaller blond boy.

Next to the portrait was another of a proud, blond man. But farther behind it lay a silver-framed daguerreotype of a dark-haired gentleman with pencil moustache and heavy-lidded eyes. It stood behind a terracotta Egyptian sphinx and a sandstone statuette of Bastet. And lying between Bastet and a mantle clock covered in red velvet was a framed cabinet card. In the photograph, a beautiful, tall blonde woman in a light-coloured dress brightly smiled. Her breast was pinned with a cascade of flowers. She stood arm in arm with a smaller dark-haired woman in dour black whose eyes were darkened with kohl and who wore a similar corsage on her chest. Head slightly tilted, she gazed at the camera sceptically. The card's bottom border bore, along with the photography studio's name imprinted in gold, the inscribed words: MARRIED 22nd of June, 1878.

As the mantle clock ticked, a paper rustled in the room. Mrs Elle Black, aged twenty-four, sat by the windows facing the street and read *The Times*.

Clad in a grey-trimmed black housedress with three-quarter

sleeves, white lace cuffs, a white bodice front, black buttons, and white cravat, she looked the picture of a proper middle-class English wife except for certain peculiarities. Her upswept hair, perhaps originally auburn, was dyed with henna to a shade of deep red and smelled of cloves, which she had added to the colouring to achieve the red's darkness. Her hazel eyes were lined with kohl, and her lips had the light paint of rouge.

Whenever deliverymen or postmen came to the house and caught sight of Mrs Black, they could not help but wonder what manner of man or men such an exotic kept company with. In conversation they found her pleasant, but eventually her black-rimmed gaze stared overly long as if she sought answers deep within their souls, and this prompt many to hastily take their leave and bid a good day.

She had just finished bottling ginger beer she'd been brewing in the basement, dusting the shelves that displayed Faedra's markswoman medals, her sterling silver tennis cup, her archery cup, the silver-framed photograph of the girls' cricket team of Miss Head's School (from which a younger Faedra, leaning on her bat, gave a brilliant smile), spot-cleaning the hallway carpeting, sweeping all the rooms, and running her mechanical carpet sweeper over the rest of the rugs.

Though there was always more household maintenance needing attendance, it was that time of afternoon where she liked to take off her apron, apply rouge to her lips, and wait by the parlour window for her spouse, Mrs Faedra White-Black.

She turned a page of her paper and read about the latest murder case reported by her favourite journalist, Helia Skycourt, and which involved the Secret Commission agents Artifice, the artificial ghost, and Jim Dastard, the animated skull. Elle had read of their first celebrated case where the duo had rid London of a dangerous re-animationist. The present article affirmed that the pair had also defeated the murderous black arts surgeon known as the Bone Stealer. Elle found Artifice being both Quakeress and a strongwoman a queer and exciting combination.

"And she's an artificial ghost," Elle said aloud, delighting in the description.

She studied the illustration of Artifice fighting zombi men in a hospital room and wondered if she and Artifice would ever meet. Faedra said the agent was staying at the Vesta, an exclusive club discreetly located in Whitechapel and which catered to those who favoured the company of their own sex. Faedra passed the club during her work as a buildings rent collector, her tenants located in the same warren. Though it was a club she and Faedra would love to patronise (as long as it wasn't terribly deviant), a membership seemed extravagant. But the club held occasional ticketed events that they could afford. Elle would like, if she'd courage enough, to then ask Artifice for her autograph.

Elle clipped the Bone Stealer case out of the paper and arranged it in her scrapbook.

She heard Faedra and Mrs Haggins speaking in the foyer and realised that her spouse had passed by the window while she had been busy pasting. She set her scrapbook aside and rose to greet Faedra at the parlour's entrance.

"You are the sweetest!" Faedra said after Elle's kiss in greeting. Being partly American, her British accent had an inflection. Her blue eyes sparkled as Elle retrieved her handkerchief from her sleeve to wipe Faedra's mouth of the rouge her own lips had left there. "Now what have I done to merit such affection?"

"By looking beautiful, Faedy," Elle said.

She loved when Faedra returned from work. Though Faedra laboured amongst the poor, resolving their tenant squabbles and investigating those who needed housing, she liked to dress prettily without diminishing colours or style like fellow female philanthropists did in order to look charitable and demure. Right then she was in a splendid blue dress that was darker than her own blue eyes. The outfit was burgundy-striped with black velvet lapels and collar and with woven burgundy buttons running down the bodice front. Atop her blonde hair, she wore a cavalier hat that was black with a silver, round medallion in the hatband's front and a fluffy arcing plume at the side.

When out with her spouse, Elle felt colourless and mousy in

comparison yet would have it no other way. Faedra's bright and friendly presence attracted the attention of both sexes and often won them especial treatment in department stores and luncheon rooms. Elle took secret satisfaction that she, out of any suitors who could be favoured, was the one married to Faedra White.

Faedra laid the magazine *The Englishwoman's Friend* on the side table, removed the long silver hatpin from her hat, and set it and her *chapeau* beside the magazine.

"Yet I look beautiful every day," Faedra pouted as she pulled off her kid gloves. "Perhaps you are placating me in advance for something you've a notion for, Elle."

"Perhaps I am," Elle said with a smile, and returned to her seat by the window. She picked up a letter. "A matter has been brought to my attention which you may agree I should apply my talents to, Faedy. Due to the urgency of the request, we should expect our letter-writer, a Miss Josefina Dufish, to visit today."

"And what matter is this?" Faedra said, approaching Elle. "How odd that she should come so quickly without an acknowledgement first from us."

"Well, though I take no fee for my services, it is still a service. No different from the demands of the tenants who've need of your attentions, whether you've time to listen to them or not. First, tell me how your week will be, dear? I know much is going on."

Faedra sat in the armchair across from the window and leaned back with a sigh.

"Such a day, Elle! I have not one but three women accusing their husbands of personal violence! I also have two families behind on payment and two more to investigate before I allow them rooms in the buildings. There's a plumbing matter, and a roof matter, as an artist is complaining of leaks into his garret. When it has not even rained, of course. And I've a woman accusing another of stealing a chicken."

"Oh, dearest! It sounds like a very busy week for you. I am so glad these workwomen respect you. The spinster rent collectors truly don't understand what married women go through and I think the workwomen are fortunate that you can commiserate."

"Well, I try to listen," Faedra said, "as father was in similar circumstances before his importing business prospered. I wish my brothers had his passion. But the women do like it that I'm married. Had we children, Elle, they would respect me even more! Now. What of this letter, darling? And when you tell it to me, sit on my lap."

"You are a silly goose," Elle said, rising to oblige Faedra's request.

When she was seated, she read the letter aloud.

"Dear Mrs Black and Mrs White-Black,

"It is with great urgency that I write you, for there is no-one else or any authority I can turn to. My name is Josefina Dufish, and I work as secretary to Mr Hardwick, the owner of Sundark Hotel, located in Chiselhurst. The hotel is the reason why I request your help.

"If you are unfamiliar with the Sundark, I will explain. Forty years ago, an illusionist built this home as a gift to his wife, a powerful occultist. The house has mechanical abilities. It can rotate and change to fit astronomical and solar predictions. It's said it can rearrange itself to work with the magnetic properties of the Earth. But it has a dark history, for houseguests disappeared in it, the illusionist's wife was driven mad somehow, and then the illusionist disappeared.

"I feel that Sundark's dark history has returned. Hotel guests are now vanishing, and they are doing so faster than before."

"Faster than—well, their disappearance is easy to explain, Elle, they didn't want to pay the bill!" Faedra said.

"It appears so, doesn't it?" Elle said. "Yet she goes on to say that the house has an old reputation for queer happenings, that here and there a guest might vanish. She had believed that history was concocted just to make the Sundark more notorious. However, the more recent disappearances seem different, perhaps caused by malevolent spirits, and she fears for herself and the guests. Thus, she must visit us immediately."

"I see. She has invited you to stay at this Sundark, hasn't she?" Faedra said, taking the letter to look at it. "No wonder you welcomed me with a kiss."

"But I kiss you when you come home every day, Faedy."

"Today you were such an eager puppy," Faedra said, smiling. "Oh! Up with you! My leg's asleep."

Elle rose and Faedra did as well. Elle returned to her seat and picked up her scrapbook as Faedra paced, pondering the letter.

"With all my responsibilities this week, I can't accompany you," she said. "But you're not off to this queer hotel, just yet. After we hear more about this business, we shall see. Sundark! I can't say I've heard or read of it, but I've not lived in England long. What about you, Elle?"

"I haven't, Faedy. But then I grew up mostly in the country and abroad."

"Well. It is Chiselhurst. It would be good for you to go; you've been an utter hermit, dear."

"It is a worthy reason to leave the house, I suppose," Elle said, smiling.

Faedra huffed. Elle looked at her curiously, knowing her sociable wife rarely liked to express displeasure. Faedra dropped the letter near her and turned for the fireplace.

"Seeing your dead husband walking about Regent St. last week has driven you into hiding," she said. "I know you'd rather avoid another experience of his phantom, but if he really were that, wouldn't he have appeared to you in our home by now?"

"Perhaps," Elle murmured, looking down at her scrapbook. "And I understand that you're cross because I haven't accompanied you out since my encounter."

"Oh, Elle! I don't mean to make light of your experience, dear."

Elle watched Faedra pick up the daguerreotype of the dark-haired man. He was elegantly dressed, slim, tall, broad of shoulders with black wavy hair. His complexion was dark, like one deeply tanned, and his heavy-lidded eyes beneath his arched dark brows had a slight slant, lending his gaze a feline air.

"I've just never been more annoyed at your first spouse than now," Faedra said.

"Oh, Faedy," Elle said.

"Are you certain what you saw was him?" Faedra demanded. "Because I must wonder how he raised himself from the dead. Surely after five years there shouldn't be much to raise!"

"It was no other, Faedy, he was a singular man. That is why I'm certain he was a phantom. Only His Royal Highness' Secret Commission may resurrect the dead, so it can't be an easy feat. As you say . . . well, we can never know for certain, but perhaps it can still be done, with his dust and skeleton. And really, why raise Valentin? He was a mere rake, though I loved him."

"Whether ghost or man, he is still a failure!" Faedra said. "For after all this time, even when you were trapped in that asylum, he had no recollection to come for you."

Elle rose and quickly joined Faedra by the mantle. She hugged her, wrapping her arms around her from behind.

"I can't say I enjoyed my time in the asylum, but it did teach me important things," she said gently. "The depths of deceit; the selfishness we are capable of, and the malice we can do. But it also taught me to recognise a true heart, which was why I ceased being mad, so that I could love you." She hugged Faedra more. "Please don't fret. That is usually *my* indulgence. You've yet to hear my complaints about Lt Montague's rooster and my continuous battle with the mechanical washer."

"Oh, Elle." Faedra squeezed her hand. "I'd gladly dismiss the whole matter if only one petty thought would loosen its hold on me. Had Valentin lived I would have been life-friend to you only, and not have all of you, as I do now."

"You bless me," Elle whispered.

She turned Faedra around and kissed her.

When their lips parted, Faedra was smiling. Elle dabbed Faedra's mouth with her handkerchief. She looked at the daguerreotype in Faedra's hands.

"In this supernatural work we do," Elle said pensively, "we've encountered too many people who see what they wish to see."

"Yes. Those manifestations, originating from our fervent minds or some lingering energy, which you call phantoms and the Society for Psychical Research calls 'crisis apparitions'.

But, Elle, after all these years, now you need to see Valentin again?"

Elle took the daguerreotype and placed it back on the mantle.

"I don't believe I do," she said. "But my eyes have spoken otherwise."

"Mrs Black, Mrs White-Black," Mrs Haggins called from the parlour door.

"Yes, Mrs Haggins?" Elle and Faedra answered in unison.

"There's a visitor here to see you, a Miss Josefina Dufish, ma'ams," Mrs Haggins said, stepping into the parlour to hand Faedra a card.

"'Doo*fish*'!" a female voice with a Caribbean accent called behind her.

"Doo-*feesh*," Mrs Haggins said sourly.

A petite African-Jamaican woman entered, curvaceous of figure and wearing a black-and-white striped dress and a sloped, silver-buckled black hat with white feathers. She carried a small, black-and-white-striped parasol and declined Mrs Haggins' offer to take it from her. Elle thought Josefina quite young, but she knew she might be mistaken about her potential client's youth. Josefina firmly shook both Faedra and Elle's hands and at their invitation sat in a chair with its back to the fireplace.

Elle moved her scrapbook and supplies out of the way, placed her chair to face the room and sat. Faedra took the armchair across from them. In this way, they formed a triangle around the parlour's turtle top table. With Josefina clearly lit by the window, Elle could contemplate their visitor's figure should anything uncanny occur.

"Mrs Black, Mrs White-Black, thank you for receiving me," Josefina said.

"I hope your trip here from Chiselhurst was uneventful?" Faedra said with a welcoming smile.

"Me carriage driver was clever and made swift time here by crossing Westminster Bridge," Josefina said.

"I'm glad you could avoid the congestion of London proper, Miss Dufish," Elle said. "I hear Chiselhurst is a very pretty suburb. Quite favoured with the well-to-do, and new houses are being built all the time in those lovely woods. Camden Town in comparison doesn't quite measure, I'm afraid."

"Chiselhurst is very pretty, Mrs Black. I see Camden Town as growing still," Josefina said.

"A very forgiving observation, Miss Dufish! Camden Town is utterly colourless. But Mrs Black likes it for its lack of surprises, and it is a very reasonable suburb for housing," Faedra said.

"Miss Dufish, I've just shared the contents of you letter with Mrs White-Black," Elle said. "I have to say it's an intriguing circumstance, and I wonder how I can be of help."

"Indeed, Miss Dufish, it sounds more like a matter for the police," Faedra said. "Sundark seems a troubled establishment, having attracted the sort of persons who've taken advantage of the hotel's supernatural reputation."

Elle had watched Josefina during their conversation while they led her to switch her attention between them. Nothing seemed out of the ordinary around Josefina or in the air. Elle decided to focus less on studying their visitor and more on what she had to say.

"To avoid paying their bills? The police thought the same, Mrs White-Black," Josefina said. "But Mr Hardwick says that *real* spirits be bearing these people off. Me mother was a healer and understood the unseen world. Living in a duppy house no scares me. But when these duppies be kidnapping people — perhaps killing them! Then I must do somet'ing."

"Killing people! Miss Dufish, how do you know? And why aren't the police more concerned?" Elle asked.

"There are no corpses, Mrs Black," Josefina said. "What can we do when there be nothing to show? But in these past weeks, I've heard and seen t'ings. People screaming. The house changing. The air feeling bad. I saw and smelled blood once, come from beneath a door and pooled on the hallway floor. I fetched Mr Hardwick, and the house changed back. The blood was gone. Dis sort of t'ing, Mrs Black, it be needing specialised help."

"When you say 'changed', Miss Dufish, do you mean the house

changes due to Sundark's mechanical movements?" Faedra asked.

"When I say 'changed', Mrs White-Black, I mean that I see halls and rooms that were not there before. Sundark moves its parts around by its machinery, that's true. Mr Hardwick, he has a passion for the engines and works on them constantly. But Sundark cannot add and remove rooms!

"First, there be extra walls, then less. The same for the steps of the stairs. The floor it be raised one moment, the ceiling may be lowered. Doors are there, and then they be gone. The changes don't stay. And worse," Josefina said, leaning forward, "I've seen people walking through them changes. People I thought not at Sundark. And I cannot tell if they really were people, or duppies!"

Elle and Faedra looked at each other.

"Only you can know, Mrs Black," Josefina said. "Truth be how your eyes work! Or so I've heard."

"Elle can see what we call ghosts, you are correct, Miss Dufish," Faedra said. "Though she views them perhaps in their true state, beyond what we understand ghosts to be."

"A haunted hotel," Elle said thoughtfully. "Yet . . . widows beleaguered by their dead and girls menaced by prankish spirits have been more my measure, Miss Dufish. I feel you may not require myself, but an exorcist!"

Josefina shook her head. "Sundark needs a truth-knower. I've seen the work of voodoo men, and who are these exorcists but the same sort of charlatans? They have no power!"

"Miss Dufish, have you any faith in religious agents?" Faedra said, smiling.

"Have you, Mrs White-Black?" Josefina asked.

"Well," Faedra said. She glanced down but still smiled.

Mrs Haggins entered with the tea tray. While Elle served tea, Josefina and Faedra fell into conversation about the Secret Commission.

"Those agents fight t'ings that threaten all of London, Mrs White-Black," Josefina said. "Why should they come for duppies in one little hotel? But I troubled meself to write the Secret Commission regardless and I received their answer. They cannot send anyone, especially when the police be doing nothing."

When she accepted her cup from Elle, Josefina put three lumps of sugar in it.

"I be at me wit's end with all the queer business at Sundark," she said. "Mr Hardwick agreed to me finding help. The duppies must go. And whoever comes to make them go, that person be staying at Sundark for free, meals and all."

"Yet out of all the spiritualists in London who could help, you contacted Mrs Black?" Faedra said as Josefina drank her tea.

"Oh yes! Unless it just be stories, I read that Mrs Black can do more than see the duppies."

"Yes, Elle is capable of more. She is also an anomalous perturbationist."

"I prefer the descriptive, 'remote influencer'," Elle said. She sipped from her cup.

"Then it's true. You move t'ings, it isn't the spirits who do so."

"I do it, yes. As do others, who unwittingly think the cause are ghosts."

"Do you eject peculiar t'ings?" Josefina said. She leaned forward. "What those Psychical Research men call 'ectenic force'?"

"'Ectenic . . . force'?" Elle said.

Josefina sat back with an air. "I subscribe to their yearly journal. They've explained it, how you levitators move t'ings with psychic fluid."

"I believe Miss Dufish is referring to 'ectoplasm', dear," Faedra said.

"'Ectoplasm'," Elle said thoughtfully. "Oh no, Miss Dufish, I do my best to refrain from ejecting."

"If she did, I would have to provide her with far too many handkerchiefs," Faedra said.

"Well! Dear," Elle said, looking at Faedra. "I believe we've heard all that is helpful."

Faedra returned her look. She put down her cup and saucer on the table.

"Miss Dufish, if you might excuse myself and Mrs Black for

just a moment?"

"I be enjoying me tea," Josefina said, smiling.

Elle wiped her cup of her lip rouge, set it down, and excused herself. She followed Faedra out of the parlour for the drawing room. Faedra closed the doors.

"Darling, what are you doing?" she said to Elle. "We could have easily given Miss Dufish our answer after she'd left."

"I know, Faedy, but I've my answer now. I would like to go."

"Not without myself," Faedra said. "This is sounding a little more dangerous, with pools of blood and such. And here I am, with domestic quarrels to mediate, and two family cases to investigate and review."

"This is why I want to go now, tonight, Faedy. While you are busy. Once I see this business through, you'll be free too and we can have time together."

She smiled as Faedra took out her handkerchief from a pocket and wiped Elle's mouth.

"No more painting your lips," she said. "I love it that you do it for me, but oh, how others think less of you for such love!"

"I don't care. The fact that I wear kohl is startling enough for those who see me. Does this mean I may go, Faedy? I'd like to see a bit of pretty countryside again. And Chiselhurst is only, oh, an hour's ride from here?"

"It is a distance of two hours, Elle, unless the horse is made to trot. I saw Miss Dufish's carriage from the window, and the horse looks healthy enough. Very well." Faedra sighed. "You may go. I know how much you miss such surroundings. I just cannot live in the dreadful, boring countryside. May I have a temporary maid come to carry out your numerous household chores?"

"Oh! I suppose you must. You know I don't like engaging help when I can maintain our household between Mrs Haggins and myself!"

Faedra pinched Elle's cheek.

"You are ever frugal," she teased. "I will pack for you."

While Faedra went upstairs to pull out their suitcases, Elle rejoined Josefina and told her the news.

Josefina was glad of the decision, and Elle decided to reserve further queries about the happenings at Sundark until she had a chance to view it and its possible phenomena. After a discussion of the fee (which Josefina insisted on; therefore, Elle suggested a widows and orphans fund that Mr Hardwick could contribute to), the conversation turned to a subject that came as no surprise to Elle. In her experience, either people entirely ignored her and Faedra's marriage or tried their best to make discreet inquiry. Josefina was nothing but direct.

"How is it, Mrs Black, that you and Mrs White-Black are married?" Josefina asked while Elle refilled her teacup.

"Do you mean how is it legally viable, Miss Dufish?"

She offered the sugar bowl to Josefina, who added three more sugar cubes to her cup.

"Correct, Mrs Black. For I can think of no church nor government that would recognise it. Not that I mind your union. You be respectable ladies, I can see. And what I also see is that you can keep your money and property. In a proper marriage, the husband owns everyt'ing, even the woman and children!"

"You have hit on it exactly, Miss Dufish. What Mrs White-Black has with me is a legal contract. The law must recognise that our contract has, like a business partnership, made legal arrangements and therefore we may refer to ourselves as 'married'; the combining of our estates for one, where we've independent rights and ownership, and our agreement of financial responsibilities, should we exercise the freedom of dissolving our union. In our case, the financial situation is all to my favour should we part. Faedra has made legal promise to provide for me," Elle said. She sipped her tea.

"Provide, even in divorce? It be sounding like the marriage reform that not be happening!" Josefina exclaimed.

"The movement is struggling, isn't it, Miss Dufish! Mrs White-Black and I were invited to participate in the petitioning, since legal unions like ours set an example of equality for traditional marriage. We certainly weren't the first to form such a union; Faedra looked to the experiences of the great American actress

Charlotte Cushman to define breach of contract and wrote the artist Rosa Bonheur, who was gracious enough to share how she and her most recent spouse created a mutually beneficial document."

"Mrs Black, if Mrs White-Black be providing by contract, did you not bring money to dis marriage?" Josefina asked curiously.

"None, Miss Dufish, I was destitute. I had been an heiress, but all my money vanished right when my husband died, shot by my younger brother in a duel. And my husband . . . shot my brother. I buried them both. I went mad as a result," Elle said. "My talents manifested. I was placed in an asylum until Faedra rescued me, three months after his death."

"Yet in the end, t'ings worked out well for you, Mrs Black," Josefina said. "Besides the madness and such."

"It did," Elle said, her eyes shining. "I am so fortunate."

Elle heard Faedra descend with two of their suitcases, Mrs Haggins following with the carpetbag. Elle excused herself so she could change out of her housedress into an outfit suitable for travelling. She stopped Faedra on the landing.

"Miss Dufish has, as rapidly as she's able, accepted the revelation of our marriage and dismissed it," Elle whispered with humour. "She's also attempting the same with the news of my madness, but it may be challenging her formidable progressiveness."

"Former madness, dear! You are wicked!" Faedra admonished in a low voice. "I do favour Miss Dufish's formidableness, however. I would welcome her as a compatriot were we in the same profession."

"Or if she were a cricket player," Elle teasingly whispered, and allowed Faedra to pass and enter the parlour.

When she ascended to the second floor and entered the bedroom, she saw that Faedra had already laid out her simple, black wool travelling dress with panelled skirt and plain bodice decorated with black buttons. Laid on the skirt was her brass chatelaine that Faedra like to call Elle's 'detecting equipage'. A brass doll's mirror, a notebook with telescoping pencil, a compact spyglass, a magnifying lorgnette, a match safe, and a

petite, brass holder of retractable tools hung from chains attached
to the curling snakes of a large Medusa-head medallion fronting
a sturdy metal clip. The longest chain on Elle's chatelaine was
of three feet with a weighted fob of brass and crystal, and this she
would wind around her small waist.

Mrs Haggins knocked at the door and entered.

"Mrs Black," she said. "Did you want anything further done
with the ginger beer just brewed, ma'am?"

"Is this Faedra's query if she might have a bottle?" Elle said,
smiling. "I had finished the bottling, Mrs Haggins, and Faedy
may have one after her dinner tonight."

While she changed, she told Mrs Haggins of the temporary
domestic help that would be employed for the week. They also
talked on house matters, such as dairy and bread delivery (since
Elle would not have time to bake that day), the items required
from the greengrocer and butcher, the cleaning of the floors,
grates, windows, and drapes, the laundry, the airing of the beds,
whether the strawberries inside the garden hotbed were ready for
picking, and what sort of meals would be cooked for Faedra.

"I'll make certain she's home and fed, Mrs Black," Mrs
Haggins said, smiling. She helped put away Elle's housedress in
the armoire. "I must say, ma'am, it's a shame you won't wear some
colour on this outing! You've a very fine plum frock, so rarely
worn!"

"Faedy knows I'll choose to wear colour again of my own
accord. And I will. I just find the black simpler!"

"That it is, Mrs Black! Though I think five years is enough time
for mourning," Mrs Haggins muttered to herself.

She left while Elle wrapped and fastened her chatelaine to
her waistband and pulled her bodice end over it, the crystal
fob twinkling. She donned her black travelling cape and black
bonnet with velvet trim before her dresser mirror. She picked up
the Vulcanite mourning brooch of a woman's pointing hand and
raised it to her breast.

She paused and thought about the apparition of Valentin she
had seen.

"Having you point heavenward does seem pointless, now," she said to the brooch.

She put the piece of jewelry back. She made certain the penny with the bullet hole she wore on a fine chain was secure around her neck, picked up her black gloves, and exited her bedroom for the stairs, her chatelaine jingling.

Faedra had given the suitcases to the carriage driver. Elle could spy the driver through the foyer's open front door, loading her baggage. On the carriage door was the lettering: SUNDARK. She rejoined Faedra and Josefina in the parlour, both discussing American politics. Here she picked up her carpetbag, and the three exited for the entryway. Elle turned to look at Faedra.

Elle smiled happily. Faedra hugged her.

"You jocund wench!" Faedra whispered in her ear.

Elle took hold of Faedra's face and kissed her. She held the kiss for a long while.

"When I return, you'll learn how jocund I can be!" she said after their kiss ended.

She turned and saw Josefina watching them with surprise. Josefina's face shuttered into politeness and she stepped outside. Elle looked back at Faedra fondly, then followed.

Josefina stood by the carriage, her parasol's handle against her chin in a pose of thought. Elle bent to caress the sculpted curls on the sphinx's head.

"If you don't resolve this 'duppy' matter in a timely manner, I will come fetch you!" Faedra said. Her cheeks were flushed.

"Yes, Faedy," Elle said, staring at Faedra. She petted the statue again.

"Mrs Sphinx, make sure Faedy is well cared for while I'm gone," she told the statue.

When she boarded the carriage, she opened the window as the vehicle departed. She waved to Faedra until she could no longer see her. Scruffy children and a barking dog ran after the carriage, the children shouting gaily. Sitting back, Elle saw Josefina studying her thoughtfully.

"You and Mrs White-Black be very close," Josefina said.

"Yes, we love each other."

"Oh, that can be seen, Mrs Black."

"Yes, but what I mean is that we truly love each other.   As man and woman would. Why, I would call Faedy 'husband' if she would let me, as she performs all the duties of such."

"Ah . . . yes, Mrs Black."

"She prefers that I don't address her so only because she thinks it makes us unequal," Elle said. "If I could just earn an income like she does, then I could be 'husband' too!"

She leaned forward, smiling.

"We hope to have children, Miss Dufish. We will pick a man."

"Mrs Black, you be an openhearted woman," Josefina said in a tolerant tone. "You be plainspoken 'til you forget that some t'ings be best left unknown."

"But I like when people know, Miss Dufish!" Elle said.

"That I can see too, Mrs Black," Josefina said with a smile.

She pulled out a small book from the folds of her striped skirt and began to read. Elle looked out the window and watched as they crossed the bridge over Regent's Canal and left slumbering Camden Town.

CHAPTER TWO

Josefina dozed off long before they'd finished crossing Westminster Bridge into South London. Elle watched the city's chaotic bustle slowly fade to quiet suburban rows and then to woods hiding large homes. She looked at her timepiece and judged that the hour and half that had passed (just as Faedra had predicted), had them well within South London's Bromley ward and Chiselhurst. She brought out her polished walnut compass and took off its cover. Inscribed on its face beneath the glass were the words: *Tempus Fugit.*

While noting the compass's reading of "North", she smelled fermenting manure adrift on the wind and heard another set of wheels and hooves on the road they followed. She peered out and saw a small wagon ahead, driven by a tall, thin man in a wide-brimmed hat. Straw remnants and a pitchfork lay in the wagon's back. The carriage driver prompted his horse and their vehicle came alongside.

"Evening, Willy!" the driver called down. "Spreading 'round more of your fine product to the neighbours, I see?"

Elle studied Mr Willy and his fragrant little wagon as Josefina woke.

"Aye, Mr Arch," Mr Willy said, turning briefly. His face was gaunt and humourless. "I'll see you back at the house."

He urged his horse to pass the carriage, and the sound of his wheels faded away.

"Oh!" Josefina said as she looked out. "That be Mr Willy, gardener for the Sundark, finishing with the delivery of his prized manure to our neighbours. We be nearly there, Mrs Black."

"Miss Dufish, can you tell me who else will be at the Sundark?" Elle said. "Of the staff and guests?"

"Many of the staff have fled, Mrs Black," Josefina said as she put her book away. "Only Mr and Mrs Willy remain, who were already serving the Sundark when Mr Hardwick came. There be two girls who help with rooms and the kitchen, and a boy with other t'ings, but like Mr Arch"—Josefina pointed above to where their carriage driver was seated—"they scurry home fast as they can go, once duties be done.

"And the guests, Mrs Black," Josefina added with a sigh. "Mr Hardwick be turning those away since the last one disappeared, but there are some who insist on staying. Dis sort of duppy business, it makes them like the Sundark more."

Elle pondered that as the driver slowly drove the carriage through a black gate, the winding drive lined with tall trees with reaching branches. One scratched the carriage, and Elle watched the branch quiver when it lost its hold on their vehicle. More such branches seemed ready to catch the carriage as they passed, and Elle thought Mr Willy was a rather neglectful groundskeeper to allow the driveway trees to go untrimmed. The carriage climbed upwards, clearing the trees, and approached a great burgundy house lit by the setting sun and made to gleam from its many art glass windows. Elle stared up the hill at Sundark.

The house stood three stories high, with circular windows of ruby glass and oriel windows with panes of stained glass. The old-gold gables displayed circles with radiating lines. The windows and sections did not predictably align nor follow symmetry, and rather than being a house mainly of four walls, had many turns, sides, and turrets. Two matching black Arabesque domes sat on fat towers, while a third smaller dome sprouted from a turret at the topmost level, its roof's tip bearing a black iron weathervane with lady's hands pointing to the four compass points. A decorative hand, mounted on the very top, raised a finger heavenward.

It was a massive home, thick and solid yet bejewelled and ornate, like a well-fed odalisque. Yet Elle thought its sensuality held complexity in its unconventional shapes, and the whole of the house delighted her eye.

"Aren't you a beautiful queen?" Elle said in admiration.

"It be a comfortable enough house, Mrs Black," Josefina said. "When it not be haunted. Oh! There be Misses Brunch and Sweetwater."

Two older women sat in the round porch by the portico. The porch's roof was a witch's hat dome, and behind the women was a long bay window paned with art glass. They waved from their wicker chairs, and Josefina popped her head from the carriage window to answer the gesture with her parasol.

"They be two of our four guests," Josefina said. She withdrew into the carriage, smiling. "If you watch the house, Mrs Black, you'll see —"

Elle felt a chill, though there was no wind within their enclosed carriage. Josefina's words ceased and the horse came to an abrupt halt. A protest from Mr Arch died on his lips as the Sundark suddenly shadowed.

Elle saw the towers and the upper two floors of the house move. They began to spin. As they did so, translucent shadows multiplied and divided, the ghosts of windows, corners, and walls tilting and flying above the house's first floor like a mad carousel on a steadfast base. Elle became faintly aware of a sustained, silent scream, felt not heard. The house whirred as if to show all its faces at once.

Janus, Elle thought.

The spinning ceased.

Elle heard the leaves flutter in the trees.

"Was that what you wished me to see, Miss Dufish?" Elle said softly, as she stared up at the house. It appeared as it had on the carriage's initial approach, solid and whole. The sun glowed on its red walls and jewelled windows. The driver urged his horse again, which reluctantly resumed its pace.

"Not quite . . . that, Mrs Black," Josefina said slowly.

Elle heard a rumbling. The two matching Arabesque domes slowly began to rotate, as the tower portions beneath them turned in the opposite direction. The round porch also moved, gently carrying away Misses Brunch and Sweetwater until the entire porch had rotated into the house and revealed its other half, which bore two men seated in wicker chairs, enjoying cigarettes. Once the rotation completed, the porch came to a stop, the towers and domes ceasing their leisurely dervish above. The weathervane slowly spun.

"I be referring to the evening mechanical turning of the house," Josefina said belatedly.

The carriage finally reached the portico and came to a halt. Mr Arch unloaded Elle's suitcases and placed them at the entrance as the ladies disembarked. After a tip of his hat, the driver swiftly mounted his seat and departed. Carrying her carpetbag, Elle followed Josefina up the portico steps for the airy, round porch adjacent.

The men rose as the women approached, and Elle saw that one was a pale, lean middle-aged fellow with a droopy moustache while the other was a young man with a smooth, golden-skinned complexion. Elle thought his features lovely—the shapes of his cheekbones and mouth—despite his reserved manner and the coolness of his light-blue eyes.

The calmness of both men indicated to Elle that they'd only been aware of the mechanical turning of the house and had been oblivious to the supernatural spinning. Though it had happened in the floors above them, she thought such a phenomenon could permeate to the interior.

Josefina introduced Elle as a 'psychic detective', the older gentleman as Mr Neville Lunt, a tins salesman, and the younger fellow as Mr Austin Washington, an American ghost-chaser. The men touched their hats, and though Mr Lunt raised his, his hand revealing a bright-gold band on a finger, Mr Washington did not.

"How do you do," Elle said. "Mr Washington, I can understand why you're here at the Sundark, but Mr Lunt, why would you stay at such a notorious place, especially when I understand that the owner even discourages it?"

"Well, Mrs Black, the nightly tariffs are quite appealing, indeed," Neville said, nodding. "Nowhere in South London can be found a more affordable place to rest one's head. And I'll say it's quite grand surroundings for the price, don't you think? Like a stay at the Palace Hotel. Although! I must mention, Mrs Black, the Sundark's service? I'm afraid it deserves a rating not worth a guidebook's mention. My apologies for saying, Miss Dufish!"

"But it be true, Mr Lunt," Josefina said.

"Well, the service, Mr Lunt," Elle said. "Yet what of the vanished guests? Don't the disappearances bother you?"

"I suppose they should, Mrs Black, but . . . oh, I'll be here only one night more!"

"Mrs Black," Austin said, and Elle noticed that not only was he beautiful and well-proportioned but quite short of stature, as they could see eye-to-eye. "I had assumed Miss Dufish had gone to fetch a medium. A 'psychic detective' sounds like one of those guises the scientists from The Society for Psychical Research don. When they expose false supernatural occurrences."

"I'm not a member of the society nor am I a medium, Mr Washington," Elle said. "For I've yet to converse with an actual ghost."

"Mrs Black, Mr Willy's come," Josefina said. "We'll have your bags brought up to your room."

Elle looked and saw that Mr Willy stood in the entryway, her suitcases in hand.

She and Josefina bade the men good evening and entered the house. Elle only had time to note Sundark's rich, red wood and the details of the foyer before she and Josefina were hailed from the parlour facing the porch Neville and Austin were presently in. Within sat Misses Brunch and Sweetwater in their wicker chairs, the parlour stove's fire pleasantly crackling. Elle saw the circular line in the wood floor that separated the moveable area of the parlour from the steadfast portion. The upper sashes of art glass behind the women were of yellow-rayed suns arcing in intervals against a blue sky, the smiling evening sun being devoured by a green lion.

"Miss Dufish! You've brought Sundark another guest, I see!" the smaller, thinner, and brighter-eyed of the two women said. Her silver hair was short and topped with a velvet green tarbouche with black trim and tassel. On the front was a black, felt cut-out of a sun, sewn on. She raised her slender hands, fluttering them in delight while her matronly companion, poised in her seat with hands clasped, smiled.

Josefina introduced the tarbouche wearer as Miss Eden Brunch and her companion as Miss Fidela Sweetwater.

"They be spiritualists, Mrs Black," Josefina said. "And admirers of the legendary powers of Mrs Sundark."

"We're not here just to admire her spirit, Miss Dufish! But to bask in it," Eden said. She lowered her voice to a conspiratorial tone. "Like cats before Bastet."

"How intriguing, Mrs Black," Fidela said before Elle could respond to Eden's surprising playfulness. Fidela had a long face and a patrician tone, but Elle thought her gaze and smile were kind. "A 'psychic detective'? Then you should know that Eden has considerable clairvoyant talent. Sundark is a lodestone and has gifted strength to her abilities, to say the least."

"Oh! Then you felt the house as it showed its faces, Miss Brunch?" Elle said curiously.

"It showed its . . . 'faces', Mrs Black?" Eden said, tilting her head with a smile.

"Like Janus would, if you will. He who is named for our January and whose two faces looked to the future and the past. And is Roman god of beginnings and transitions."

"And thus of doorways, gates, and such!" Fidela added, seemingly pleased. Eden continued to smile, her eyes darting as if studying Elle's face. "Very good, Mrs Black! I don't know about 'faces', but oh, gateways and such!"

Elle looked at Fidela expectantly, feeling like a child awaiting how to solve a figure at the blackboard.

"You almost have it, Mrs Black," Fidela said, smiling. "Almost!"

Before Elle could query further, she heard a clatter. Pulleys spun, chains moved, and cables swiftly wound deep within the house.

"Heavens," she said. "It sounds like a tiny train is arriving."

"It be arriving, but is no train, Mrs Black. You must come see," Josefina said to Elle, smiling.

Elle quickly excused herself from the ladies and followed Josefina. Mr Willy stood in the hallway with her bags and waited patiently, if not a little sourly. Josefina led her down the entry hallway to a bright, hexagon-shaped reception area. Elle looked up and saw the dome of the skylight three stories above, its art glass of a sun's black centre radiating gold lines. She dropped her gaze to regard the recess in the wall directly before them. Thick cables of two pairs ran from a half-concealed ceiling mechanism to where an ornate, wrought-iron housing surrounded a hole in the floor. A huge counterweight on one pair of cables swiftly dropped from above. Elle watched it fall out of sight into the hole and knew from the rumbling beneath their feet that something was arriving.

"It's an ascension chamber!" she exclaimed as the iron roof and then ascension room itself rose out of the floor. It was a long, four-sided enclosure of panelled wood and plate glass. As the room came to full stop, Elle saw a large man's figure move within.

"It is, Mrs Black, but Mr Hardwick doesn't allow it for guest use anymore. It goes only to the depths below," Josefina said.

The door of the chamber slid open, then the housing's gate, and out stepped a man with thick, black wavy hair and sideburns, his dark brows drawn down in a scowl over his grey eyes and Greek nose. Elle thought his chin so resolute it could strike an anvil. His barrel chest strained the buttons of his shirt, dirtied with grease, and his rolled-up sleeves revealed dark-haired arms equally soiled. In one huge fist he gripped a leather apron, hung with tools, and Elle saw that his braces hung carelessly from the buttons of his rough, workman's trousers.

But when he stepped forward, his body swaying, Elle realised that despite the upper strength of the man, his hips and legs betrayed a weakness. She didn't wish to stare and discern the manner of his bodily defect, but she thought his might be a long-time lameness.

"Josefina!" he said as he lurched towards them. His voice was the equal of his huge chest and echoed in the reception area. "My Caribbean bird! Flown from this rock of black sun and now flown back?"

"Mr Hardwick, I be gone only for the day," Josefina said tolerantly.

"Day, hours—minutes! Like our vanished guests, you took no time to pack, but who could say that once out of sight of Sundark and having regained your sanity, you would deign returning to such a mad place again?"

"Humph! If and when I leave you, Mr Hardwick, you'll be told it, clear as bells ringing in your ears! I brought help with the duppy business; this be Mrs Elle Black," Josefina said. "And dis man, Mrs Black, be Mr Hardwick, owner of the Sundark."

"Well! Yet another clairvoyant!" Mr Hardwick's fierce gaze bore down upon Elle before she could give greeting. "We've had a great many like yourself come stay. And just as quickly leave, if they had their wits about them. *Then* there are those who haven't any sense at all. I'm sure you'll let us know which sort you are."

"I—" Elle said.

"We're also short on staff so don't expect any mollycoddling," he interrupted. "It's every guest fending for himself, though meals are served when it's expected. It will be like camping, Mrs Black! Have you ever been? Except here, you'll be 'roughing it' in a hotel."

"I have 'roughed it', Mr Hardwick, in my father's archaeological sites. But unlike in Egypt, can we expect clean linen, towels, and water?" Elle asked. "And no wild animals?"

"You'll have those things you've mentioned, Mrs Black, but I can't promise that some wild presence won't cause this place to spin tonight."

"'Spin', Mr Hardwick?" Elle said.

"Willy, what are you standing about for? Have Mrs Black taken to her room!" Mr Hardwick ordered.

"I would, sir, but I haven't a room number yet," Mr Willy said.

"That, I'll be fetching," Josefina said.

She excused herself and left for an adjacent office. When she opened the door, Elle saw a large study with a drafting desk and shelves piled with rolled plans. Some drawings were pinned to the walls. She spied a very tidy desk with a flower in a vase and wondered if it was Josefina's.

"Mr Hardwick, a hotel seems a fascinating business to own," Elle said. *For such an uncouth man*, she mentally added.

"Pah! It's the business that came with the house, since Sundark had three previous owners, including the builder. The man before me thought this would make a splendid hotel."

"I take it you're interested only in Sundark's mechanical aspects?"

"Its mechanical secrets are more like it, Mrs Black. There is nothing like the Sundark."

"Oh, it's a most complex place, indeed. And purposed for supernatural workings, I understand! But why are the spirits so active now, Mr Hardwick?"

"Ask them, Mrs Black! I know nothing of their nonsense, nor do I care to. Are you fancying you've seen some already? We shouldn't believe things we see here. I've decided to ignore all hallucinations."

"Yet, Miss Dufish said that you're certain ghosts are carrying away your guests. Isn't that your belief?"

"Questions, questions! That's all you little birds ask, are questions," Mr Hardwick said. "Then, if smart birds, you fly away." He made shooing motions with his hands. Josefina returned, holding a key.

"True, but like many a little bird, we must return for that seed that was strewn, Mr Hardwick," Elle said with a raised eyebrow. She turned with Josefina to take her leave.

"Josefina!" Mr Hardwick said. "Before you accompany Mrs

Black up to her room, I'd like you to tell me where you hid my notebooks again."

"Mr Hardwick, you be piling papers all over them like a dog burying bones! I will find where they be." She turned to Elle and handed her the key. "I will join you and Mr Willy before the great staircase, Mrs Black."

Mr Willy took that as his cue to depart the reception area for the drawing room, Elle following, while Josefina and Mr Hardwick stepped into the office. As Elle entered and crossed the drawing room, her chatelaine lightly jingling, they passed a great mirror hung over the fireplace's ornate overmantle. Elle stared into it, watching the room's reflection—the windows, chairs, and shadows. She saw no apparitions and nothing seemed amiss, but she vaguely felt that something was.

"Is there a mistress of the house, Mr Willy?" Elle suddenly said.

"Wot?" Mr Willy said. He'd exited the room for the staircase area and stopped in surprise. Elle stood in the drawing room's exiting doorway.

"I only ask because, well. It's only proper that I should also greet the mistress. One moment, Mr Willy," Elle bade. She heard Mr Hardwick's laughter in the reception area as she brought out her compass. The needle quivered, giving a reading that deviated from "North" by twenty degrees. She watched it struggle to return to "North" and then looked up upon hearing Josefina step into the drawing room from the reception area.

Josefina crossed to her, smiling. Elle saw the air distort around the small woman.

Elle focused her mind. She took mental hold of Josefina's bodice and drew her forcibly forwards. Josefina's feet flew off the carpet. Elle dropped her just as the mirror over the mantle shattered outward. She watched the event slow to her perceptions, her gaze witnessing every shard of glass that flew. She formed a mental "soup ladle" and flung all the pieces back, sending them to smash against the mantle's wall.

Josefina scrambled to her feet and threw her arms over her head as the bits of glass Elle had not caught fell about her.

She ran towards Elle.

"Mrs Black!" she cried. "That was you?"

"I was the one to grab you, Miss Dufish, but the mirror's explosion is an occurrence I can't explain."

Josefina looked at her and then at the pile of glass at the foot of the fireplace. Mr Hardwick rushed across the room.

"What just happened *here*?" he bellowed.

Elle informed him as simply as she could, though Mr Hardwick stared blankly when she described pulling Josefina out of harm's way with her mind. After making certain Josefina was well, Elle quickly excused herself, claiming fatigue after the journey. She firmly dissuaded any further queries. In frustration, Mr Hardwick turned his attention to the state of the mirror, which then held only a large shard of glass. Elle saw Misses Brunch and Sweetwater peer into the room from the reception area.

Elle might have considered joining the discussion and inspection that would result, but whatever force or intention that caused the mirror to explode had long departed, and she murmured that opinion to a concerned Josefina.

Elle turned to look at Mr Willy, who still stood with her cases in hand. He appeared both confused—perhaps disbelieving of what he had just witnessed—and strangely, also conniving.

At Elle's scrutiny, he hefted the cases and resumed walking. She felt a familiar ache begin at her temples and followed him.

CHAPTER THREE

As she and Mr Willy climbed the great staircase, Elle reached into her carpetbag and found one of the self-heating cans Faedra had squirreled away for her. Taking the plain, tin-plated steel object in hand, she twisted its bottom, breaking a barrier within that would cause two chemicals, copper sulphate and powdered zinc, to combine. She quickly wrapped the can in her cape as the resulting exothermic reaction heated the water chamber within.

Thus, by the time they reached the second floor and her room in the middle of the hall—as indicated by her key, "Number Four"—which she thought a very nice bedroom with a four-post bed, chest, armoire, dresser, and reading table by the windows, she had a freshly brewed and piping-hot feverfew tea to treat the headache threatening. Mr Willy dropped her suitcases, touched his hat, and left without a word.

Josefina knocked and entered while Elle was seated at the table, bonnet and cape removed and sipping her tea. Her compass sat before her. Josefina wrinkled her nose at the bitter tea's wafting scent.

"That be feverfew in your cup, Mrs Black?" she said.

"Yes, Miss Dufish, a very small amount, brewed with lemon balm and chamomile."

Elle replaced the cover on her compass as Josefina approached. All the while, the arrow had quivered between 'North' and a deviation of twenty degrees.

"Mrs Black, you be ailing?" Josefina exclaimed. "It's your head, me know it!"

"Oh, but once I've the tea the pain goes away! It was the sudden application of my abilities, Miss Dufish, that brought this sort of condition on. When I'm more prepared, my head doesn't hurt at all!"

"Which is why I come to thank you," Josefina said. "How did you know what would happen, Mrs Black?"

"I didn't, Miss Dufish," Elle said. She shook her head. "Though I knew *something* was about to occur, and to get you away from whatever that was."

"Mr Hardwick and meself looked all about the drawing room, and even peered inside the chimney. We can find no reason for the mirror shattering. This house may tremble from its movements, Mrs Black, but to have glass fly like that? And me take from your answer, you no saw the duppies?"

"I'm afraid I did not, Miss Dufish." Elle smiled, enjoying Josefina's reversion to stronger Jamaican speech.

"Well! It be another strange happening for Sundark."

"Miss Dufish, forgive me for wondering, in case Mr Hardwick is a mere bachelor. And one wouldn't be surprised, with his manners. But . . . is there a Mrs Hardwick?"

Elle noted Josefina's pause.

"She be gone before I come work for Mr Hardwick, Mrs Black," Josefina said solemnly. "But yes, he be married. Or was."

Josefina then informed her that dinner would be served in half an hour.

Elle quickly finished her tea, placed her suitcases on the bed, re-did the bun of her hair to further relieve the ache of her head, and emerged to explore her surroundings. The second floor hallway had wallpaper of a recent style, the colour being tan with a bronze fleur-de-lis pattern. The gaslight fixtures were pleasant yellow orbs of blown glass that also seemed modern. At the one end of the second-floor corridor was a gated opening into the reception area proper.

When Elle looked down, she saw the ascension room, still sitting on the main floor. She found no devise that would summon it, except for a box in the wall that revealed a speaking tube. A door next to it—one Elle thought might be for servants—led to the open-air corridor circling the reception area. Above was a similar corridor connected to the third floor. She assumed both led to the servants' wing.

Elle counted eight rooms on her floor plus a ninth door at the very end, painted a shimmering old-gold. She walked down to try the doorknob, thinking the door too small and narrow for a room's entryway and found it firmly locked. She then departed for the staircase in the middle of the hall.

Down below, she neither heard nor encountered anyone and assumed all were in their rooms, preparing for dinner. As she explored, she passed her hand along the panelled walls and plate-glass partitions. She looked about the gas-lit parlour, drawing room—where all the glass had been swept, the mirror's frame still hanging with its remaining shard—the woefully empty solarium, the music room, and the library. In each one, she held up her brass doll's mirror (inscribed with: "Tripoli Hotel Grand Opening, Seneca Falls 1875"), which Faedra had given her, and studied the room's reflections. She discerned nothing remotely extraordinary.

The house, to her critical eye, lacked the needed attention of maids and housekeeper. Cobwebs dangled from a few light fixtures. Dust lingered on carpets, floors, and shelves, revealing clear patches, indicating that furniture and objects had recently been removed. The library especially was on its doleful way to matching the solarium with the destitute state of its shelves. Elle found a folded, illustrated pamphlet on one dusty shelf and realised that it was promotional literature for the Sundark Hotel. She read:

Welcome dear Traveller to The Sundark, where Crowns of Europe, wealthy personages, and distinguished persons of title were invited into this most extraordinary of manses to be amazed and enthralled by the secrets of our Unknown Worlds, and in profuse admiration, showered both the mystical Heric and Abigail Sundark with jewels and treasures for the formidable demonstrations of their preternatural powers.

She opened the pamphlet. Beside each small illustration of a room in the Sundark, she read a description:

"The Blue Room, otherwise known as the Left Tower, was where the masterly illusionist Heric Sundark designed his many escapisms, such as his diabolical water torture act whilst thrust up, nearly naked, in chains, and his deadly box of impalement, from which he'd emerge unscathed, even when bound hand and foot inside the monstrous instrument. Though the secrets of his workroom are now gone, the Blue Room is suitably furnished for the needs of our masculine and distinguished clientele, who might indulge in emulations of the masterful pursuits of its former inhabitant.

"The Right Tower, also named the Gold Room, was the fecund sanctum of Heric's Circe-like spouse, Abigail Sundark. She, who could summon such wild spirits to her séances that participants were nearly made sacrificial lambs to their orgiastic demands. Mediums and spiritualist circles are invited to gather in this powerful chamber for rest, especial workings, and sidereal adventuring.

"The Third Tower, smallest of the three and most intimate, was said to be the cell where Abigail called upon the attentions

*of pagan goddesses, with altars fragrant with incense and laden
with offerings to such deities as Hekate and Aphrodite. Guests who
have stayed in this, our most celebrated of rooms, have witnessed
fairy lights, heard sweet music play, and been visited by fluttering
touches and kisses by beautiful spirits.*

Elle rolled her eyes.

"Had I a third tower for the alchemic meeting of blue and
gold, I'd do more than summon fluttery lips," she said. Such a
consideration made her think of Faedra, and she decided that was
enough of reading provocative advertising copy. She tucked the
pamphlet into her dress pocket and exited the library.

"Hekate," she said thoughtfully.

While she pondered, Elle lightly rapped Sundark's walls and
revelled in their thickness. She admired the joining and fitting
of the beams and supports, the carving of the balustrades, and
the sun-like presence of the glowing, blown glass fixtures. Like its
exterior, the interior had elegant attributes but was robustly sturdy,
and Elle presumed such construction was to accommodate the
Sundark's movements as well as hide the machinery.

And it's very muscular activity! Elle thought. *To move such
rooms and floors as these.*

"You're quite strong-boned," she said, looking up at the
darkened dome above the reception area. She entered the dining
room.

A long table was set for seven people. Elle straightened the
tablecloth and chose one of the mismatched chairs next to the
table's head. As she pulled it out, she noticed a pinched-face
woman observing her from the entry of a narrow hallway—one
possibly leading to the kitchen. The woman's sharp eyes were
focused on Elle's chatelaine.

"Good evening," Elle greeted.

"Good evening, ma'am. I'm sorry I disturbed you; I was
surprised to hear a chatelaine," she said.

"Perhaps you thought I was the new housekeeper?" Elle said
lightly.

"That's not possible, ma'am."

Elle looked at her humourless face. The woman retreated into the narrow hallway.

"And your name is?" Elle called.

"I'm Mrs Willy, ma'am. Dinner will be served soon."

With that, Mrs Willy disappeared.

Elle heard women lightly conversing outside in the reception area. Fidela and Eden, who wore a crown of silk flowers, entered and greeted her. They sat down at her side of the table while Neville Lunt and Austin Washington entered and took seats across from the spinsters, leaving the spot opposite Elle empty. Austin wore his hat, and Elle thought that since the others ignored his impropriety she would let him be.

When Josefina and Mr Hardwick appeared, Mr Hardwick claimed the chair at the head, lurching towards it without aid of a cane, while Josefina sat down across from Elle. Mr Hardwick had washed and changed, and Elle thought his profile striking with his thick hair tamed and his neck sporting a properly turned collar and grey tie.

He greeted her gruffly and stared at her.

"As further explained to me by Miss Dufish, it's now my understanding that you are not just a clairvoyant but a witch," he said.

Elle looked at him, wondering if she was being complimented or taken for the devil's companion. She thought such a statement from the present owner of a supernatural house was rather archaic.

"I prefer the appellative 'remote influencer', Mr Hardwick," she said.

Mr Willy approached and laid down a platter of roasted beef for Mr Hardwick to carve.

Once a slice of beef was placed on Elle's plate and she'd sawed a portion to put in her mouth, she wondered how such a stalwart British dish could be so woefully mishandled. Her slice tasted like shoe leather. The gravy bowl contained a greasy and watery concoction. The boiled potatoes had black bits she carefully cut away, the bread was as chewy as India rubber, and the burnt biscuits were doughy in their centres. The expected roasted parsnips and carrots to accompany the beef never arrived. Instead, she received a limp dollop of braised lettuce for her greens with a cooked caterpillar hidden in the leaves.

Elle slowly went about her meal, recalling asylum days of worse fare. Her host, however, took to his dinner with a harsh and thorough resolve as if he sought to demolish his food, or at least the needs of his stomach. Mr Hardwick's fork and knife rang against his plate as he filled his mouth. Josefina ate daintily and with a leisurely pace perhaps designed to inconspicuously leave behind the indigestible on her plate. Neville picked swiftly at his food like a searching bird, flicked black potato bits aside, and ate any edible discoveries just as quickly. Austin chewed some things, ignored others, and took a long while inspecting the contents of the breadbasket, which he eventually monopolised, slathering his choices with thick butter.

Eden, who sat next to Elle and nibbled, seemed to find the elements of her meal as entertaining as an adventurous expedition into the wild. She chittered to herself as she picked her potato apart, and Elle thought the incoherent words a happy sound, impolite though it was for Eden to have a conversation solely with herself at the table. She wondered if Eden had ever spent time in an asylum.

"Mrs Black, I must wonder," Eden suddenly said. "But have we seen you on the stage, perhaps?"

"The stage?" Elle said. She took a sip from her water glass, hoping it didn't contain dishwater.

"Well! Your eye cosmetics, Mrs Black! So . . . dramatic!"

"Yes, Miss Brunch, I do apply the kohl heavily. And not because I trod the boards. I would call such earnest application a superstition of mine."

"A 'superstition', Mrs Black?" Fidela asked in even tones from next to Eden. Despite Fidela's cultured voice, Elle did not find her query cool or patronising, but gentle and pleasant.

"It's a custom of Egyptian women," Elle said, "to apply kohl liberally to guard their eyes against the gaze of the Evil Eye, or any directed malevolence. Eyes are where we view souls, after all. Silly, I know, to protect myself in such a manner, but I do find it comforting."

"*Surma*, as it's known in India, is indeed a protecting agent, also applied to the eyes of children," Fidela informed the table with a delighted smile. "Even men wear it!"

"Considering what *we* witness, Mrs Black, you should use all the Egyptian spells at your disposal!" Eden said.

"What does your husband think of such embellishments, Mrs Black? Or would that be your second husband? Are you remarried? And who is it that you're mourning?" Mr Hardwick suddenly inquired, his questions like shooting bullets.

"Mr Hardwick, how like a little bird you are with your many questions! I've been in mourning for my parents, my brother, and my husband. And yes, I have remarried, and to a very beautiful and loving woman," Elle said.

Mr Hardwick stared at her and chewed. He turned to look at Josefina, who merely smiled at him. He then returned his attention to Elle again. He put a potato in his mouth with his knife and ate it.

Neville looked perplexed, his droopy moustache angled, while Austin focused on his buttered bread slice and ignored her. Eden giggled, apparently delighted by the confusion that had descended upon the table. She then exclaimed over the compote of apples that arrived, served by Mr Willy.

When dinner was done (the compote passing muster by Elle's estimation, though she thought the apples old), Josefina announced that the stargazing demonstration in the Sidereal Dome would soon occur. Everyone rose, expectant and eager, and made their way out of the dining room. Neville grabbed the last bread slice from the basket and wrapped it in a blue handkerchief, then stuffed it in his pocket.

"What is this Sidereal Dome, Miss Dufish?" Elle said.

Mr Hardwick stoically led the way up the great staircase, his climb laborious. The other guests, apparently accustomed to this nightly entertainment, chatted as they leisurely followed him.

"It not be visible from the front of the house, Mrs Black, but on the third floor be a grand room, nearly big as a ballroom, with a dome that folds back to reveal the sky," Josefina said.

She excused herself to walk ahead and join Mr Hardwick by the banister as he climbed. He took Josefina's arm in congenial spirit when they reached the second floor, but Elle could see that he leaned on her.

"The Sidereal Dome is one of the splendid mechanical achievements of Sundark," Fidela said to Elle. "A personal observatory to the heavens."

"And this dome opening occurs every night?" Elle asked. "I looked out this evening and thought that clouds were gathering."

"Well, it's said that no matter the weather, it's always a clear sky above the Sundark!" Neville said. "The sorcery of Abigail Sundark supposedly saw to that. But then the dome shouldn't open when it rains. Has it ever, Mr Hardwick?"

"I've never known it to," Mr Hardwick called back. They reached the third floor. At the end opposite the ascension room's gated access was a set of ornate double doors with baroque scrolling and reliefs of the sun and heavenly bodies. The wall surrounding the doors was painted a royal blue, setting it apart from the tan wallpapering of the rest of the hallway.

With this here, where does Abigail Sundark's Right Tower and Gold Room lie? Elle wondered, recalling the gold door on her own floor.

The doors mechanically opened at Mr Hardwick and Josefina's approach. The darkened corridor within curved, perhaps to accommodate the tower. Elle followed everyone into the darkness and heard the echo of their footsteps and of her own jingling chatelaine in a very large space. The other guests were following the faint, gold lines and star shapes on the floor. The designs subtly glowed, and Elle recognised them as the twelve zodiacs.

She gathered with the rest in what seemed the room's centre, glanced up into the darkness, and noticed the glowing figures above, curving within a great dome.

"The skeleton man is bright tonight! Oh, look, Fidela, how he and his crow glow so," Eden exclaimed.

"Him! I'm thinking that lion is exceptionally clear, the one eating the sun," Neville said.

"I believe they are all quite distinct tonight, Mr Lunt. My, look at the winged beings," Fidela said in wonder.

"It's just a matter of our eyes having become well adjusted to this darkness, that's all," Austin said. "We have viewed this quite a number of times and all that artwork above is becoming pretty familiar by now."

Elle studied the ceiling outlines that formed clear drawings to her, and thought they did glow more, when compared to the fainter stars on the floor.

We stand on the sky, but above us . . ., Elle thought.

"Are alchemic formulas," she said softly.

She heard a heavy sound reverberate, and then organ music, light and sweepingly airy, began to play. It was a Vivaldi concerto, its notes dancing, and before she could look about to see who was playing so deftly, the dome cracked open, revealing a sliver of clear and twinkling night, then more stars in the black firmament as it continued to open. The bright face of the moon peeped and slowly emerged. Elle glanced at the raised faces around her, noting that everyone was present, which meant the music playing was self-acting. Mr Hardwick stood where the first cast of moonlight fell fully upon him, his upturned gaze searching.

The music rose, playing in earnest, and Elle felt the floor abruptly move. Fidela caught her as she sought her balance. They began to rotate as the dome's halves widened further. The opening formed a perfect circle of the sky, the edges packed with clouds, as if pushed aside.

"What did I tell you?" Neville said. "We've a hole to the heavens."

The music reached a crescendo as the dome opened completely. Everyone applauded.

"My," Elle said, clapping too.

"There! Jupiter!" Eden cried, pointing at a bright star near the moon.

"Big fellow!" Neville said. "Let's find Venus, and maybe we can name most of the constellations before the rotation's done."

The organ music played as Eden pointed out more discoveries. The floor continued to slowly move clockwise, and Elle marvelled at how the night above spun. She felt Fidela touch her arm.

"I'll tell you what happened to the missing guests, Mrs Black," Fidela said in a low voice. She gestured to the moving chamber and smiled, her gentle tone reverent. "It takes one of faith to understand the possibilities here."

"Is this a spell chamber, Miss Sweetwater?" Elle asked.

"Oh yes. This house sits on a sacred place, Mrs Black, sacred to a goddess. And its movements are workings; workings toward the transcendence of our bodies. Abigail Sundark achieved this through her husband's machines. She discovered how to transport herself . . . *there*."

Elle looked up at the stars Fidela pointed to.

"You're saying . . . Mrs Sundark also disappeared?"

"Not disappeared, Mrs Black, only gone ahead!" Eden suddenly interjected. Elle started, not realising the smaller woman was near.

Eden drew closer and motioned for Elle to lean towards her.

"Mrs Hardwick was said to have done the same," she whispered in an arched tone behind her hand.

Elle glanced to where Mr Hardwick was. The moonlight edged his distinct profile as he gazed skywards.

A shooting star suddenly blazed across the sky. Eden jumped, looking delighted. Elle put a hand to her chest, having never seen one so big. Everyone applauded.

"Soon, we shall be given the doors to the quintessence. Doors! That will transport us to Saturn, to Venus!" Eden cried, her arms lifted to the heavens.

Elle saw the smirks shared by Neville and Austin, but Mr Hardwick did not scoff. Instead, he stood quietly, his gaze still contemplating the skies as the rotation came to full stop. The last note of the organ trailed off. Elle heard the deep reverberation return as the massive dome began its laborious process of shuttering closed. Gradually, they were enveloped in darkness.

"And now, guests of the Sundark, the Sidereal Dome demonstration be concluded," Josefina announced. The doors to the brightly lit hallway mechanically opened.

While Josefina showed the others out, Fidela joining Eden, Elle approached Mr Hardwick.

"I feel very fortunate that I could witness this performance of the Sidereal Dome, Mr Hardwick. Thank you for keeping the machines in working order so that we may have this experience," she said.

"You needn't thank me, Mrs Black. It is the Sundark's doing."

"Do you mean to say that the Sundark runs of its own accord?"

"It does, just like a woman's heart, Mrs Black. I'll tell you there's so much of the machinery—the endless mechanisms and many of them hidden—that it'll be a while yet before I discover and document all of them. But I may never understand how some of the engines do what they do, and why. If Heric Sundark had sold himself to the devil to make this place come to be, I'd believe it."

"Sundark's machinery sounds very impressive," Elle said.

"It is," Mr Hardwick said. "It's why I wanted the house . . . but more so did my wife, who was a spiritualist. Sundark inspired her pagan heart. This room, especially, was her favourite place to dwell."

"I would have liked meeting Mrs Hardwick," Elle said.

"Well, when you find her!" he suddenly snapped. He swivelled and lurched for the exit.

Josefina left the door and approached Elle, who stared thoughtfully at Mr Hardwick's retreating back.

"She was one of those who disappeared, Mrs Black," Josefina said in a low voice. "Here, in Sundark. It be a delicate matter."

"Because he doesn't know if she merely left . . . or is truly dead," Elle said.

"Or is disappeared into the house," Josefina said, her face sad.

Elle glanced up in the darkness and discerned the faint gold lines of the figures above. The lion continued to eat the sun.

"Departed for Venus, you mean," she said.

Josefina gave a long sigh and shook her head.

When they left the Sidereal Dome, Austin was in the hallway erecting a tintype camera with a bellows body on a wooden tripod. He aimed his instrument down the corridor, the front of the box bearing four lenses. Neville stood at his door in the middle of the hall and bade the spinsters good-night. He waved the same to Elle and Josefina and entered his room. Mr Hardwick was nowhere to be seen, though a laborious shambling could be heard down the staircase.

"So this is the manner in which you catch ghosts, Mr Washington!" Elle said when she and Josefina approached. Eden and Fidela departed down the stairs as Austin positioned himself on his stool. "I didn't realise you were a spirit photographer."

"I am not one of those, Mrs Black," Austin said haughtily. "Tricksters who alter photographs."

"No, Mr Washington be posing the duppies with a paper moon," Josefina said lightly.

"I do no such thing, Miss Dufish!" Austin snapped while Elle suppressed her laugh behind a hand. "I'm in pursuit of a sincere photographic capture of a true apparition."

"I think it's quite clever to have a multiplying camera," Elle said. "Then you may have four images of the same subject."

She looked at the worn camera with its metal development tank fixed to the box's bottom and recognised it as the same sort used seaside, in the parks, or at fairs to make the very affordable souvenir tintypes the less well-to-do could indulge in; especially with a giant paper moon backdrop, as Josefina had said.

"Yes, for I intend to keep two for myself and send one each to the British and American Societies of Psychical Research."

"It not only multiplies photographs but it be an automatic,

Mrs Black," Josefina said.

"A 'repeater'," Austin said.

"There be several plates already inside." Josefina pointed at the main body. "When Mr Washington squeezes his rubber bulb, a suction arm be grabbing a plate and lifts it for the photo, then drops it into the tank there. He can take many duppy portraits in a short time. They just don't be sitting still for him."

"It's gratifying that you remember my explanation of how my sort of photography works, Miss Dufish," Austin said.

"Would you happen to have any such portraits to show now, Mr Washington?" Elle asked.

"No, Mrs Black," Austin said. He fidgeted with the bulb in his hand. "But only because of unfortunate mishaps."

"The camera fell once," Josefina said. "Another time, his plates be inserted backwards. And many portraits be of the walls or empty hall. Or of the dark."

"These events, Miss Dufish," Austin said in a chilled tone, "do happen faster than my shutter can expose. I'll not fail tonight. The Sundark is the most kinetic, preternatural locus I've ever investigated. I'll get the proof I want, and it'll make me a very distinguished man to both the American and British Societies. Good-night, ladies."

They bade him good-night and descended, but Elle glanced back to where Austin sat behind his tintype camera, his bulb in hand.

"You may want to remove the lens caps, Mr Washington," she said.

Austin grimly reached around his machine and yanked the caps off his multiple lenses.

As they made their way down, Elle admonished Josefina for her teasing.

"Really, Miss Dufish," she said.

"He be having airs," Josefina sniffed. "Me not one for tolerating his sort of rudeness! Especially from a man who not be liking his true self."

"Yet he seems very determined," Elle said.

"They be all mad! If I could make them leave, Mrs Black, I would. Oh, I'd be taking a stiff broom to them stubborn backsides!"

"Your broom would not work on Mr Hardwick," Elle said.

"No, that be certain."

"Miss Dufish," Elle said when they reached the second floor. "Mr Washington seems convinced the phenomenon will happen in his location. But such occurrences don't happen just on the third floor, do they? The blood you saw, for example. Where did that appear?"

"Oh, Mrs Black, I will show it to you."

Josefina led her to a room at the end of the second floor hallway where, she explained, the last victim had disappeared. She pointed beneath the vanished guest's door. Elle glanced to the side and noted that the gold door stood only a few steps away.

"When the duppy stuff be happening, t'ings be different, Mrs Black. I be witnessing a door . . . over the true door, and that terrible spill, smelling like real blood!"

She then opened the door and showed Elle the room. Despite the darkness, Elle could see that the interior was torn down. The floor, walls, and even the ceiling had their panels and walls removed, revealing only framework.

"When this guest disappeared, Mr Hardwick had enough of the vanishings," Josefina said as Elle studied the room. "And the police too! They all be wanting to know if the house be full of chutes and traps and secret passages. But the workmen could reveal nothing! I be very disappointed when I saw this. And Mr Hardwick too."

"Miss Dufish, how many guests vanished before you came to me?"

Josefina took a deep breath.

"I come work for Mr Hardwick nearly four months ago. Me father be an engineer like Mr Hardwick, so I know what a builder needs in a secretary. I be seeing the duppies meself only two months later. A guest vanished, and I thought he be running from his bill. One month more, another be gone, same like the first.

Then last week . . . we lost Mr Chipperings."

Josefina quietly shut the door.

"And how did Mr Hardwick explain these losses to you?" Elle said.

"He said it be either of two t'ings," Josefina said solemnly. "One, they ran away. Two, the duppies took them. And meself, I be thinking after the last disappearance that they be taken permanently."

"That was indeed what you wrote, Miss Dufish. Now I need to know how the phenomenon happens. Whether it's random or possesses the whole house."

"Yes, Mrs Black. I think it be the whole house," Josefina said thoughtfully. "Because if we seek each other during the happening, we be lost in it—the changes to the house I had described to you. And then it be over just as it had started."

"Then what I'll do is remain here on the second floor," Elle said. "Thank you, Miss Dufish."

Elle turned with Josefina and saw Eden in a room across, a door down from where they stood. She watched them with a wide, curious eye.

Eden smiled at Elle and slowly closed her door.

Elle requested a pot of hot water to brew coffee grounds she'd brought and retreated to her room next to the missing Mr Chipperings'. She retrieved the Sundark pamphlet from her dress pocket and placed it on her dresser. Then she went to her suitcases and opened them.

One held her clothes while the other was outfitted with stitched leather pockets, casings, and straps that lined the sides and stored her supplies. Several of the straps held more of the self-heating cans Faedra loved to prepare for her. Elle saw that three were of feverfew tea, and four were of coffee. She searched in her carpetbag for the second can of tea Faedra would have placed there and found a white paper bag. When she opened it, it contained six pieces of chocolate.

"Oh, darling Fae'!" Elle said happily. After such a dismal dinner, the candies were a welcomed sight. She set one chocolate aside.

She also found her letter-writing kit with a note from Faedra ordering her to write her every day. Elle placed the kit by her chocolate on the table and returned to her suitcase. After unpacking her press pot and tin storing her coffee grounds, she unsnapped the casing that held her portable police lantern. The black iron box had a thick, plate-glass front and handle on top. The back door, with its metal loop for hooking on a belt, held a reflector.

Elle pulled out long-burning candles from another pouch, secured one inside the lantern, lit it, and shut the door. A strong beam of light emitted.

She then packed her carpet bag with more candles, a ball of string, three rubber balls, her knitting, and brought that, her lamp, a chair, and the small nightstand out into the hall. She placed everything at the ascension gate's end and took a seat where she could easily view the gold door down the corridor.

Nearly an hour later, her requested pot of hot water had not arrived. To Elle, it seemed just as well Mr or Mrs Willy didn't come down the servants' corridor or ascend the main stair because then they might witness her mentally juggling her rubber balls and possibly douse themselves in fright.

Elle sent the orbiting balls one last time down the long hallway and then back to herself, arcing all three in a juggling motion— though their orbits had begun to decay and erratically travel— and then finally dropped them in her lap.

She gave a deep breath and patted her face with her handkerchief. Her exercises with mentally lifting weights or performing dextrous manoeuvres with objects were something Faedra insisted on, especially when unexpected psychic exertion seemed to be the cause of her debilitating headaches. Elle detested exercise practice thanks to her ungainly performances in school calisthenics, but being married to a sports enthusiast meant she would have to routinely exert herself, like it or not.

She had even advanced in her lifting efforts to levitate Faedra for a short while, but she'd yet to achieve that without great concentration or strain to herself.

"I've quite a ways to go before I'm flying about on a broom," she said. She decided to return to her room and sacrifice one of the self-heating coffee cans to the night's vigil.

After enjoying her chocolate and preparing a coffee, Elle stepped back out just as Fidela emerged from Eden's room. She wore a dressing gown, shawl, slippers, and a large cap. She held a spoon and a small cobalt bottle with a familiar yellow label. It was a freshly opened bottle of Mrs Winslow's Soothing Syrup.

Elle fixed her gaze on the bottle, and Fidela, surprised, looked to where her attention lay.

"The house moves at night, Mrs Black," Fidela gently informed. "Around the witching hour, I believe. The entire level shall do a full rotation and perform again near dawn. It was exciting the first few nights, but now Eden and I must partake of a drop to help us sleep through. Oh, But I see you've made a place in the hall . . . with a bright lantern! I could leave you the bottle if you'd like?"

Elle stared at the bottle Fidela offered. She could practically taste the syrup.

"No thank you, Miss Sweetwater," she finally said. "I've other remedies I use now. For sleeping."

Fidela nodded, smiling, and they bade each other good-night. Fidela entered her room next to Eden's, at the end of the hall, while Elle returned to her camping site. She resolutely took a sip from her coffee can and looked at her compass on the nightstand's top. Its quivering motion between 'North' and a deviation of twenty degrees remained the same. She placed her coffee by her compass and fetched her knitting from her carpetbag. She was working on a pair of fingerless gloves, and though she'd already made a lovely blue pair for Faedra, she anticipated having a substantial amount of gloves to give to widows and orphans come wintertime.

After two and half hours of knitting, purling, casting off stitches, and seed stitching, she was ready to lay her needles down to switch to her tapestry needle and whip stitch the edges of the second glove. She'd already risen twice and walked the hallway before returning to her work. She didn't know which of the spinsters was snoring, but she suspected it was Fidela. As she contemplated the corridor, its gaslights steadily burning, she debated preparing another coffee and perhaps eating one more chocolate.

Suddenly, she felt a change in the hall's atmosphere, the air vacating and fleeing up her skin like sand struck by lightning. As the hairs on the back of her neck stood on end, the needle of her compass spun.

The gaslights died. The hallway swiftly darkened with only her lantern beam showing. She hugged herself from the rapid chill that pervaded the air. With a great rumble, the house began to rotate.

Then, within the wavering beam of her lantern, she saw the hall distort.

The gaslights suddenly relit. Elle looked around. The hall was dimmer, and the lights flickering feebly inside blue glass. They weren't gaslights, she realised, but candle flames. The wallpaper was gold and blue. The hall's direction still led to the gold door, though its sense of up and down seemed skewed. Elle took hold of the nightstand and marvelled that she should feel tipped just because the hall appeared so. She heard the Sundark move, its machinery a distant, faded sound to her ears. Though she could barely hear it, she still felt the solid rumbling through the soles of her feet.

I'm still here, not elsewhere, she thought. *And I can't discern these phantom walls from the true.*

She took a deep breath, the air smelling of thunderstorms.

"This is a very sophisticated phenomenon," Elle whispered. Her heart beat frantically.

She saw a woman move in the dark hall.

Elle swiftly lifted her lamp and shined it upon the figure. She saw her back, her long black dress with layered crinoline skirts and black lace cape wafting behind. Her dark hair was in loose, wild sausage curls that fell to her cape-covered shoulders. She moved as one running to the gold door, but her pace was slow. Elle saw the shimmer of the metallic threads in her embroidered lace, the glistening of oil in her hair, and the white of her fair skin. Elle picked up a rubber ball and flung it at her.

Her nervous aim was wide. The ball missed and went through the phantom wall with its candles and wallpaper of blue and gold. Elle heard it strike the true wall behind the pervasive manifestation. When the ball reappeared on its rebound, she seized it with her mind and threw it again at the woman in black, who just then opened the gold door. The woman stepped through and shut it behind her with a click. The ball struck the wood and bounced away.

"Oh!" Elle exclaimed in frustration.

She heard a man scream, the sound chilling her bones. She looked up, thinking it came from the third floor. The house continued to rotate, but the phantom hall remained. She realised she couldn't make her way to the source of the cry while still confused by what was or was not a manifestation. She knelt and reached into her bag for her ball of string.

She saw a man's trousered legs walk past her, his braces hanging.

Elle straightened and gaped at a shirtless man with a thick, fringe beard and dark hair, his arms muscular and his back broad. His hands were in fists. He walked as the woman had run, as if slowed inside the time or memory in which he was suspended. Yet his stride was purposeful.

Elle heard another person descend the staircase with a clatter and then land in the middle of the hallway. Josefina staggered to her feet, dressed in a cap and dressing gown and carrying an old brass candleholder. It shook in her hand when she saw she was in the man's path.

"Mrs Bl—*eeeeeee!*" Josefina screamed. Her breath snuffed her candle.

Elle threw her ball of string. The loose thread sailed through the air, and she mentally drove it through the striding man like an arrow. Josefina dropped the candleholder and caught the string that shot through his body, her eyes as big as saucers.

Whir, Elle thought.

The suspended ball rapidly unravelled, whirring string around the man. She pulled it tight with her mind and watched the string slice through his corporeality. His body slowly fell apart and disintegrated just as he reached Josefina. The entire phenomenon collapsed around them like transparent ice, rapidly melting. Her lantern went out. The hall fell into pitch-black, and she heard the house's movement finally come to a stop.

The gaslights reappeared with a sharp hiss. As they glowed, they revealed globes of yellow glass. The wallpaper was of the tan fleur-de-lis pattern. Elle ran towards Josefina, who still held the string. It led to a wet, tangled mass and a gently rolling ball on the floor.

"Miss Dufish! Are you harmed? And did you look at his face? Was he someone you might recognise?" Elle said, touching her.

"Me—me hardly gave the face a look, me being more startled by the fact that he be *naked*, Mrs Black!" Josefina gulped.

"Oh, he was merely shirtless, dear!" Elle said. "But why are you on this side of the house in the middle of the night?"

Josefina grabbed her arm.

"Somet'ing's happened on the floor above," she said.

When Elle ascended to the third floor with Josefina, she saw Mr Hardwick standing before Neville's open door, staring in. Mr Hardwick was still dressed, his tie loosened and his shirtsleeves rolled up.

He grimly turned, ignored the two women, and lurched quickly to the ascension room's end. He opened the servants' door. As he departed, Josefina left Elle and quickly followed him.

Elle entered Neville's room. It was fully lit, his nightclothes still laid out on his bed. An open book with its paper marker lay beside them. Two suitcases with big buckle fastenings sat open, as if he'd been packing them. The bread he had taken away from dinner was on the dresser. He was nowhere to be seen. Elle turned around, retrieved her doll's mirror, and looked into it.

She surveyed the entire room through her mirror, and discerned no presence or lingering distortion that might tell her what had happened in the room.

She abandoned her mirror and studied the floor. Unlike the gelatinous mess encumbering her former ball of string, there were no remnants of similar phantom corporeality. The floor was well swept. Neville had stored a small broom by the door.

Elle took a breath. She looked at the armoire and mentally clicked it open. When no body fell out, she went to her knees to look under the bed and found the space clear. Then she exited.

She finally noticed Austin's camera and tripod sitting near Neville's room, apparently moved from their previous location with the stool left behind. A door two rooms down was open and well lit. She approached and looked in.

Austin was busy washing several photographic plates in a tray of water on his bed. He still wore his hat, though he was in waistcoat and shirtsleeves. He glanced up, startled, then looked down at his work again.

"If you'd like to look, Mrs Black, I have something," he said distractedly.

"I would, thank you Mr Washington," Elle said, watching him carefully. She entered the room. Several tintypes were stood up on the dresser and table. Some were of the present guests, one was of Mr Hardwick with Josefina, and three were of Josefina alone, posed in different parts of the house.

"Your camera was standing before Mr Lunt's room," she said as Austin dried a plate in his hands with a cloth. She studied his hands, rolled-up sleeves, and then the water in the tray, spying no evidence of blood and therefore of violence.

"Yes. The phantom activity started and I rushed to take this." He held the plate up for her to see.

Four identical images were exposed. Bright fires floated and surrounded the sharply distinct figure of Neville Lunt inside his room, held aloft like one in the grip of invisible assailants.

Elle could spy past Neville to where his open suitcases lay. His face was terrified.

"You opened his door . . . and then took this photo?" Elle slowly asked as she stared at Neville's face.

"No, his door was shut. At least it was shut, once the activity started. I'd—I'd never seen anything like it." Austin gazed blankly. "The walls and door disappeared, and it was like staring into a huge window . . . displaying this. He seemed suspended like that forever, Mrs Black."

Elle watched as he patted his pockets, searching for something. He spied what he wanted, lying on his dresser. He retrieved a pair of small shears and began carefully cutting the plate of Mr Lunt.

"I heard a tarnal racket!" Austin continued. "When the walls and door returned. It was as if a great fight was happening, like with bears, or tigers. And then it was silent and I tried his door. It opened and . . . all was as it was before."

"Except Mr Lunt is no longer here."

"Yes. That too."

"Could you have aided him somehow, Mr Washington?" Elle quietly asked. "Reached in perhaps, while the walls were gone?"

"Reached for him? Mrs Black, I—these manifestations that you see around him? They were blue! Bright-blue fires! They surrounded me too. God help me, I thought I was done, just like Neville. All I could do was squeeze the bulb." Austin put his work down on his bed and rubbed his face like someone trying to wake from sleep. His eyes were wide with memory.

Elle saw his coat tossed on the bed. She lifted one sleeve and studied the back and shoulders for the touch of phantoms. The coat appeared bereft of viscous substance, like Austin himself.

"I would like to show you something else," Austin said. He went to his table and pulled back a dark cloth, revealing a tintype of a woman. Elle quickly picked it up. The woman in the black lace cape with crinoline skirts looked directly at the camera as she leaned on the overmantle in the drawing room. Her black hair was a mass of loose sausage curls.

"Mr Washington," Elle said sharply, "I thought you said you

had no success in taking portraits of Sundark's apparitions, yet here is one."

"Mrs Black, she was just this woman standing in the drawing room, not speaking to me. I thought she was some queer, spiritualist visitor in strange old clothes, but . . . now I believe that she *is* one of Miss Dufish's 'duppies'," Austin said. "I didn't suspect at the time. I offered to take her photo and she didn't decline. Once I took the photo I happened to look away, and then she was gone."

Austin pulled back the cloth, revealing more tintypes.

"Here are three more. These are people I've seen who didn't answer when I spoke to them. So I photographed them."

Elle looked at the three individuals in antiquated hairstyles and clothes. The small doughy man with a fringe beard and the elderly woman in severe bonnet and dark clothes stood while being photographed, but the young girl in a plain bodice and crinoline skirt sat at a window table, hands folded and her expression soft and mild. None had looked at the camera.

"But I still think," Austin said as Elle carefully picked up each tintype, "that these may be real people. They may look like they're from our grandfathers' time, but we are in the English countryside! I've seen elderly folk about who still dress like that old woman there. She and the man merely walked away, but the young girl disappeared like the lady in black."

"Walked away? In the conventional manner, through the door?" Elle said.

Austin rubbed his forehead fretfully.

"No, not really," he finally said. "Through the walls. But I thought, perhaps they slid some secret—"

"Mr Washington, how can you not consider these proof of the apparitions?" Elle said, incredulous.

"Mrs Black, they don't look like phantoms, do they? They look just like you and me! And anyone could say I had them dress in those old clothes. The Society of Psychical Research would laugh me out the door!"

Elle turned back to the cut tintypes laid on Austin's bed.

She stared soberly at Neville Lunt's horrified visage, his body stiff as if held fast by the amorphous fires for his last, living photo.

"Are these tintypes of Mr Lunt enough proof to validate your pursuit, Mr Washington?" she said.

Austin shrugged.

"I don't know," he said. "I'll need more."

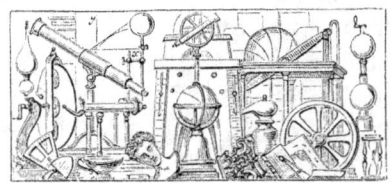

CHAPTER FOUR

My Darling Fae',
You will be proud of me, Faedy, I refused a dose of soothing syrup
offered to me, tonight! I hadn't a drop in nearly four years since you
made me stop its use and in turn, you stopped smoking cigarettes
to encourage my abstinence. I'm surprised that I can still desire it.
How correct you were, that despite its ability to quiet my headaches,
it has an insidious hold upon the body, just like gin!

Tonight, the house had a manifestation. It was quite powerful as
I could not separate its particles from that of our own surroundings.
Per Miss Dufish's description, the phantom occurrence involved
the house itself and the figures of persons. The male phantom I
witnessed had admirable cohesiveness, but it was a simple matter of
dispelling its corporeality with several wounds of string.

Whilst preoccupied, I could not witness its concurrent event,
a floor above, that supposedly bore away Mr Neville Lunt, a tin
salesman. He is nowhere to be found. Mr Austin Washington,
a ghost chaser, had photographed the event, and in viewing his

tintypes it appears that phantoms in the shape of fires—described as blue— had taken hold of Mr Lunt. Mr Washington did not see where Mr Lunt and these supposed entities vanished to.

If you did not know (for I doubt these are present in America), blue lights, or fires, are thought to be the spirits seen floating along corpse roads. However, I will withhold opinion on what "bore" Mr Lunt away until I learn more. Is he truly gone? I suspect the worst, but as you know with things inexplicable to us, there's just that small chance for the opposite conclusion. I at least believe that the phantom occurrence I had personally experienced did come from some person's, or thing's, will. For what purpose, I've yet to discover. And such a question leads me to consider what I saw at Regent Street, the week ago.

Though it has been five years since Valentin's death, perhaps I've still some heart-matter to address. For a long while, I understood that I was alive, and he was not. How many times have we witnessed this in the bereaved woman who catches sight or sound of her husband, child, or cherished friend once again? Seated nearby and seen from the corner of the eye, fleetingly touching her hand, or invisibly warming her side? Such experiences console the hearts left behind. Perhaps the guilty, we survivors, need such assurances too. For I am so happy with you, Faedy. Happy until my heart is an expansion, shining and pure. Perhaps I've a little guilt about that.

Your Loving Wife,
Eleanor

Morning was bright and breezy with songbirds twittering amongst the sun-dappled trees and fragrant flower bushes. After a lacklustre breakfast of burnt bacon, cold toast, tasteless broiled fish, watery tea, runny "hard-boiled" eggs, and a few other disappointing items, Elle departed Sundark with Josefina in the hotel's two-wheeled trap. They were headed for Bromley Town, where Josefina would mail Elle's letter and purchase supplies, and Elle would, at Josefina's suggestion when she'd queried the secretary about Sundark's origins, visit Mrs Hemrold Speckings, widow to the engineer who helped build Sundark. Within Elle's velvet black reticule, she carried Austin's tintypes.

While Josefina drove, Elle admired the blue sky and trees, marvelling at the lack of smoke and yellow discolouration in the air. She was determined then, more than ever, to continue her frugal practices until she and Faedra could afford a seaside holiday. She watched a policeman pedal towards them on his velocipede. He touched his helmet as he passed.

"Only one constable will come to investigate Mr Lunt's disappearance?" Elle asked. "Now that breakfast is done, of course."

"They be weary of the vanishings, as much as Mr Hardwick and I," Josefina said.

"Perhaps you are unaware, but Mr Washington was successful at photographing the phenomena that took hold of Mr Lunt."

Josefina glanced at her in astonishment.

"That man! He said nothing at the breakfast table!" she exclaimed.

"It may be he was still getting used to the idea of his success," Elle said. "And Mr Hardwick's black mood cast a rather daunting cloud over our abilities to converse."

"Is the photograph . . . a fearsome t'ing to look upon?" Josefina asked.

"I believe it is," Elle gently said.

Josefina returned her attention to the road, her face sorrowful. Elle pondered the likelihood of Neville still being alive, somewhere. She liked being open to any possibilities during a case, but right then she felt that sharing such a thought would be a false hope.

"Miss Dufish, I have been wondering. How did you come to be on the guests' side of the house, last night?" she queried.

"Oh, Mrs Black, I be forgetting to tell you about the night movements of the house," Josefina said. "When it started, I thought I should join you."

"You came by the servants' corridor to the third floor?" Elle said.

"I did. Me room on the servants' side be on the third floor.

Mr Washington's seen me in me nightclothes enough times, with all this duppy business. But then the changes happened, and then . . . the scream. I saw Mr Washington frozen with fright before Mr Lunt's door! I rushed down for you."

"That was very courageous, Miss Dufish, especially when the manifestation so thoroughly bewildered our senses."

"I be regretting bringing you to this evil house," Josefina said.

"Nonsense," Elle said in surprise. "You sought help, Miss Dufish, and you want an end to this so that you may have a peaceful life. I will do all I can."

"I hope Mrs Speckings be giving you the answers you need, then," Josefina said soberly. She brought the horse and trap to a halt before the garden gate of a thatched cottage with white walls and flower boxes, where a slender, old woman in a large sunbonnet tended to a rose bush. She straightened and waved to them.

Mrs Specking's maid brought tea into the brightly lit parlour overlooking the cottage's rosebushes and stone birdbath, where several small birds noisily bathed. A squirrel came boldly to the window box and peered in.

Elle turned her attention from the idyllic scene to gaze in delight at the pretty biscuits the maid set on the table before her. After the disappointment of breakfast she was still quite hungry. Though she had a hastily scrawled letter of introduction in Mr Hardwick's heavy, broad hand, she was still a queer visitor to Mrs Speckings and therefore sought to set her hostess at ease by sharing the experiences of her own marriages. Her early loss of Valentin earned her the appropriate noises of sympathy, and thus she turned the conversation to the matter at hand.

Elle picked up a biscuit and bit into it. It snapped loudly between her teeth.

While Mrs Speckings poured out the tea, Elle discreetly checked her teeth with her tongue to see if they were still whole.

If I should fling this biscuit to the squirrel, it would surely strike it dead, she thought.

She mustered a smile while she masticated.

"In answer to your question, Mrs Black," Mrs Speckings said once she filled their cups. "My husband helped build Sundark not only because it paid well but because the notion of a mechanical house that was also a celestial observatory, following the motions of our heavenly bodies, deeply intrigued him. Now, Mr. Sundark was the designer and inventor. He gave my husband plans to follow that one could hardly believe would work. Yet somehow they did, and once a design was finished Mr. Sundark destroyed each plan to ensure no one could duplicate the machines. Despite the peculiar aspects of the project, I believe my husband took great pride in helping to bring such scientific vision to realisation."

"Mrs Speckings, was the very location of the house taken into consideration?" Elle asked. "Its direction and alignment, perhaps?"

"Strange that you should ask, Mrs Black, but yes. And such a fuss it raised with the local folk. Yet Sundark needed to be built where it was for optimal viewing of the stars. People just didn't understand."

"Yet, what were they protesting? Did Sundark block a cow's path?" Elle said. She picked up a pink petit four from the platter, tasted it, and found it very dry. She drank her tea.

"Oh, that you should say that! I wish it were so. Sundark did obstruct something, Mrs Black, but the locals called them 'spirit paths'. Not just one path, but three of them."

Spirit paths, Elle thought. The ancient paths taken by funeral processions to the cemeteries; a ritual walk meant to ensure that the dead would not return up those paths to haunt the living. But the paths had an older history, not well understood by modern minds though perhaps still known amongst elder folk. The paths were also said to be the travel lines of fairies.

"You mean the corpse roads, Mrs Speckings. Such shouldn't be obstructed," Elle said.

"Oh, Mrs Black! The churches they linked no longer stand,

and were gone long before Sundark's building. The cemeteries may remain, the little of them you can find." Mrs Speckings offered Elle more biscuits.

Elle accepted one with a smile.

"Mrs Speckings," she said when she'd laid the biscuit down by her cup. "I've read that the Sundarks had entertained many guests, some of whom were illustrious. It was a house meant to be enjoyed by many."

"It is that sort of house, Mrs Black. I'd even told my husband I thought it less a home and more an elaborate theatre, except that we guests—for we were invited to a few of those parties—were no longer the audience but become players in the spectacle." Mrs Speckings set her cup down on her saucer. "I'd always found it . . . uncomfortable."

"You are referring to the demonstrations of powers by the Sundarks?"

"Their presentations were unsettling, Mrs Black, if not impressive, but I refer to . . . well, I'm not certain. One didn't just visit the Sundark. People became mesmerised by the house. Guests would beg to stay for longer."

"The house is very unconventional yet singularly beautiful. Perhaps the Sundarks anticipated such infatuation in their creation. The house has rooms enough for a castle," Elle said.

"I can't imagine feeding and caring for that many guests, but such stays were encouraged," Mrs Speckings said. "I'd heard Abigail Sundark herself say that everyone's presence gave the house life."

Elle then took that opportunity to show Mrs Speckings the tintypes. She laid out the one of the woman in black, and her hostess looked at it.

"This is Abigail Sundark," she said coolly.

As Elle pulled out the tintype of the young girl, Mrs Speckings took it from her hands.

"Minona!" she said in a hushed whisper. "This is Minona Hodges. Oh how I mourned her when she disappeared!"

"Who was she, Mrs Speckings?" Elle asked.

"She was Heric Sundark's ward! The child of Heric's distant cousin, who perished, with his wife, in a boating accident. Minona came to live at Sundark and then became Heric's secretary. More like an assistant, I believe. Minona never spoke of her work, but she was privy to his illusionist secrets, in order to help him build his escapist devises."

"You and she were fond friends," Elle said.

"Oh yes. I was such a young wife, Mrs Black. Like you, I married at nineteen too. Minona was a year younger but oh, how I adored her. So sweet and kind was she! It broke my heart when she vanished." She laid the tintype carefully down. "If Minona had run away as Abigail Sundark said, she would have at least written me. Minny would know that I needed to know she was safe and well."

"What do you think happened to her, Mrs Speckings?" Elle asked softly.

"She's dead," Mrs Speckings said abruptly. Her mouth turned down in sorrow, and her eyes filled with unshed tears. "I never doubted it. One of those two had surely killed her."

Josefina came for Elle just as tea was done and Elle was touring the flowering bushes with her hostess. They bade Mrs Speckings farewell. Back in the trap, Elle retrieved her small notebook by its chain, twisted her retractable pencil open, and wrote down what she'd learned.

She reviewed her tiny notes:

As shared by Mrs Speckings, widow of the Sundark engineer.
The mysterious events that occurred when the original owners were present, in the following order—
House party, one guest disappeared.
Family friend visiting, disappeared.

Elle pulled out the tintypes and studied the one of the male apparition Austin had photographed. He was a man approaching his late thirties, portly built and wavy of hair with the fringe beard fashionable during his time. His pale eyes with their faraway gaze seemed thoughtful yet kind, and his relaxed mouth held no sternness.

Heric's solicitor and old school friend, Mr Wellows, Elle thought, recalling Mrs Speckings' identification of the photo. She looked at the tintype of the old woman.

She thought this woman, with her white hair, lined face, and trimmed bonnet, also seemed receptive and friendly in demeanour. Per Mrs Speckings, she had been Heric's aunt. Both Mr Wellows and the aunt, Mrs Speckings had confirmed, vanished while staying at the Sundark. Elle returned her attention to her notes.

Family member, aunt to Heric, staying on at Sundark, disappeared.

Mr Sundark's ward and assistant, disappeared.

Wife thought to have gone mad. Perhaps sent away, or disappeared.

Mr Sundark never seen again (fled, or disappeared).

Josefina glanced curiously at the notebook and tintypes in Elle's lap. Elle then explained what she'd learned from Mrs Speckings.

"Mrs Speckings was a lonely young wife, isolated in dreary Chiselhurst," Elle said thoughtfully, "with only older wives to socialise with. Therefore, her one confidante was a sweet child living with two very strong-willed individuals. When Minona Hodges disappeared, Mrs Speckings could only think that the cause was murder."

"There was an investigation?" Josefina asked.

"Oh no. No-one would listen to the accusations of a young wife of nineteen. I would know."

"What do you think, Mrs Black?"

"I think Mrs Speckings' suspicion was correct. But as to the crime, I just don't know by whom," Elle said. "Perhaps what happened then is somehow cause for the vanishings now."

"It be making no sense to meself, but you be the expert, Mrs Black," Josefina said. "And now that we know of this poor girl, do you believe . . . the duppies be murdering the rest?"

"I'm afraid those are my suspicions, Miss Dufish," Elle said soberly.

Josefina swallowed and nodded. "We be half a mile from the house now."

Elle pulled out her compass and took off the cover.

"What is it you see in your compass, Mrs Black?" Josefina asked curiously.

"A steady reading of 'North', for now. Miss Dufish, when you wrote me, you said that Sundark rested on possible 'magnetic lines'."

"That be what is said of the Sundark."

"Miss Sweetwater also mentioned that Sundark was a lodestone. Each time I'd witnessed a deviation in my compass you had been near. But right now that's not the case. This rather acquits you of being the possible magnetic force that's manifesting these dangerous duppies."

Josefina looked at her with wide eyes.

"I . . . be glad, Mrs Black," she said, returning her attention to their horse.

"Oh, but dear," Elle added as she patted Josefina's arm, "you're not ruled out yet."

They arrived at Sundark by midday, the policeman's velocipede nowhere to be seen. Elle disembarked before the portico with a small, covered basket Josefina had given her. Josefina then drove on to put the horse and trap away.

Elle saw Mr Willy in the hall as she entered, carrying suitcases in both hands. He looked at her warily, then shifted his gaze. She was about to ask who was leaving when she gave the bags a closer look. Seeing their large buckles, she realised they were Mr Lunt's suitcases.

Mr Willy ignored her and quickly disappeared through a door in the reception area.

Elle was halfway up the grand staircase for the second floor when she met Austin coming down. His golden complexion was wan, and dark circles were beneath his eyes. His ever-present hat was on his head.

"Luncheon, Mrs Black," Austin said. "There's certain to be tongue and calf's head."

"Oh . . . I ate while out, Mr Washington," Elle said. "I assume the constable interviewed you about Mr Lunt?"

"That's right. It seems I'm the first to witness the actual vanishing. And my photograph helped support my witness. If this incident finally reaches the Secret Commission, the Society for Psychical Research is sure to take notice! Did my other photographs help in your query?"

"They did." She fished them out of her reticule and handed them to him. "But as these were duplicates, Mr Washington, I left the one of the young girl, Minona Hodges, with Mrs Speckings, who was quite fond of her. They were friends, forty years ago, when Minona disappeared."

"Then . . . then they are apparitions. Very well." Austin stared at the tintypes in his hands as Elle pointed each out and named them. He offered the one of Abigail Sundark to her.

"You'll want this back then," he said.

"Whatever for?" Elle said in surprise.

"Why, to do whatever you mediums do, to speak to the dead. Workings . . . summonings. Misses Brunch and Sweetwater are up in the Gold Room right now, conducting such. If you try to summon Abigail Sundark, would you do so after luncheon? When I can ready my camera."

"Do you mean the two are in Abigail Sundark's Right Tower, this minute?" Elle said.

She bade Austin keep his tintype of Mrs Sundark and hurried up the stairs.

The gold door on the second floor was ajar. Elle heard a

woman's faint voice echo down the dim, narrow spiral staircase. She entered and began to climb, holding her chatelaine still. As she wound around and around the spiral case, the voice emitted long sounds, each note dragged out to an accompanying one struck on an instrument. Light beams, shining through arrow slits, lit her passage. She heard a gong sound just as she reached a duplicate gold door, also ajar.

She peeked in. The circular room with the high dome roof was bright with dust-speckled light shining from large, round windows of art glass. The mouldings and frames were painted blue. The space was sparse, the shelves empty. Eden sat cross-legged in the sanctum's middle, dressed in white silk, Arabian bloomers, and a long, silver-embroidered white robe. She wore a small, white turban.

Elle glanced above and saw the dome's blue mural filled with stars and a black sun in the centre. Though the chamber had the heat of sunlight, Elle felt that a vibration, peculiar to clairvoyant people, also activated the atmosphere. She looked at Eden Brunch.

Eden's silver hair topped by her silk turban seemed to glow. Elle thought that Faedra's blonde locks would whiten as beautifully when older. Elle, with her dark hair, doubted she would emanate such dignity of age but more the haggard look of one past her prime once the grey hairs set in.

Eden opened her bright eyes and smiled serenely at her.

"Mrs Black! Oh, how good of you to join us," Fidela said from a window seat. She held a small mallet. Beside her were a tiny bronze gong, a small pile of books, and a toy xylophone. "Eden has just concluded attuning herself to the great quintessence."

"I do sense such achieved equilibrium," Elle said as she stepped inside, "rarefying the air. How I wish the same for myself. It has been upsetting losing Mr Lunt."

"Upsetting?" Eden exclaimed. "When he'd received the favour of Sundark's chthonic patroness? The Key-Bearer had deigned he conjoin at last, as pure essence with her own mother, the star-strewn aether." She raised hands to the blue dome. "He is now where we are not."

"'Key-Bearer'?" Elle said.

"Oh yes. Have you guessed now, Mrs Black? And you had thought 'Janus'," Eden said, her tone wry.

Elle pondered her words.

"Very well, Miss Brunch. If Mr Lunt is 'there', where are we?" Elle asked.

Eden rose from the floor.

"As she of the triple ways would have us. We are betwixt and between," she proclaimed.

Eden's lordly regard held a superior certitude. At that moment, her small, silk-clad form radiated. Eden's presence was amplified, Elle thought, by the room itself.

Elle refrained from picking up her doll's mirror to look about. Then Eden pointed at Elle's basket.

"That smells of food!" she said.

Embarrassed, Elle tried not to hide the basket.

"Luncheon!" Eden then announced. She passed Elle, her chin in the air, and stepped for the door. As Eden exited, Elle felt the room deflate. The barometric shift from rarefied expansion to a rapid flatness made her feel like a dwindling balloon.

Oh, so this especial chamber shan't work to amplify myself, then? Elle thought, resisting the sensation of dullness that threatened to diminish her. She raised an eyebrow at the Gold Room.

Fidela rose to pack her things in a basket. She smiled to herself, seemingly oblivious to the room's invisible change. Elle spotted the title on a small book Fidela stored away: HEKATE.

Elle recalled what she'd read in her parents' antiquity books.

"Miss Sweetwater," Elle said. "I've reflected on what you said when we first met. And now, Miss Brunch has duly informed me. You were correct, I shouldn't have thought of Janus when I saw Sundark's faces. For Hekate is of three faces, a tripartite deity and patroness of crossroads."

"Indeed, Mrs Black, you now have it!" Fidela said, pleased. "For she is of that liminal place; between that which is now done and is yet to come."

"As . . . Miss Brunch had said. Yet . . . how did you two come to the conclusion that such a deity presides here?"

"Oh, Mrs Black. You're not familiar, then, with Abigail Sundark's literature? She was a most celebrated occultist and servant of the tri-formed goddess. You may read her writings on Hekate recounted in *The Gnosis*."

Elle's brow knitted. She'd never cared for the occultist publication, *The Gnosis*, preferring some objectivity with supernatural subjects, like Helia Skycourt's articles in *The Times*. Fidela smiled and patted Elle's arm as she passed. Elle turned.

"Miss Sweetwater, I do recall that Hekate, if appeased properly, protects us from our restless dead," Elle said. "Were you aware that the house stands on not one, but three spirit paths?"

Fidela paused on the steps, still smiling, but Elle thought the expression hesitant, as if Fidela were weighing the information given her. Then her smile widened.

"What a powerful alignment," she said.

Fidela descended. Elle heard shuffling outside. She turned to one of the windows and saw a person's shadow briefly move for above. More scurrying was heard up the outside wall.

A hatch opened in the dome ceiling, and in the bright sunlight, Josefina's shadowed face peered in. She held her small parasol at the ready.

"Miss Dufish!" Elle exclaimed.

"Mrs Black!" Josefina surveyed the room. "Are Misses Brunch and Sweetwater well? Mr Washington said they be here, and they still not come for luncheon."

"Oh, they are descending now. Miss Dufish, did you intend to surprise a duppy?"

"If fire duppies can be surprised, then that be what I'm doing." Josefina handed her parasol down, entered through the hatch, and carefully stepped down the shelving, which Elle realised doubled as a ladder.

"You've seen Mr Washington's tintype of Mr Lunt, then," Elle said while she helped Josefina down. "I'll ask the next blue flame if it can be caught unawares. In speaking with Misses Brunch and

Sweetwater about Mr Lunt, they seemed hardly affected by his loss."

"Well, they be spiritualists, Mrs Black, believing in flights to Jupiter and such." Josefina landed on the floor.

"Mr Washington hardly seems moved either, and I doubt he has beliefs about ascending to Venus."

"That man," Josefina muttered under her breath. She slid a panel of the wall aside and turned a knob within. Elle heard the hatch swing closed with a slam.

"Mrs Black," Josefina said when she turned around. "I know you be investigating. And you told meself that no-one is above suspicion, not even the kind Miss Sweetwater. But you show no more sympathy for Mr Lunt than the others! I only be pointing that out."

"True. I've learned to set most of my feelings aside to concentrate on investigation. Perhaps everyone here also believes they're investigating." Elle pointed to the previously opened hatch. "I assume you walked the roof from another location?"

"I did. The Left Tower with the Blue Room be near my wing."

Elle heard rumbling. The Gold Room jerked slightly and then began to rotate. Josefina held her parasol and looked about warily. After a moment, Elle went to one of the round windows and looked out at the changing scenery.

"We missed the morning rotation while in Bromley Town," Josefina said.

"Perhaps the blue spirits will not return. Until someone decides to leave," Elle said, watching the trees go by. "Just as Mr Lunt tried to do."

Josefina looked at her with wide eyes.

"Mrs Black, you be correct. The last three guests were taken before they be departing the Sundark!" She shook her head in amazement.

When the house's movement ceased, they left the Gold Room with its dust-speckled light for the dimness of the narrow stairs.

"Does Mr Hardwick reside near Heric Sundark's tower?" Elle asked as Josefina led their descent. "In the old master rooms?"

"Mr Hardwick would be sleeping there if he be not below in Sundark's machines, as he is now."

They exited the gold door. Josefina shut and locked it with a small, gold key, turning it a full rotation before pulling it out. She turned to Elle.

"We may see you at dinner, Mrs Black?" she asked, smiling.

"Yes, Miss Dufish." Elle held up her basket. "And thank you."

Josefina nodded, smiling, and left by the grand staircase.

Five minutes later, Elle was standing at the ascension chamber end of the hall, still sussing out the nature of the tube in the wall and how to engage it. She finally pulled down a lever and spoke into the tube.

"Is this a calling tube?" she said into it. She paused to listen.

"Perhaps of the sort the manors use to call down to the kitchen?" she said. She listened more.

"I would like to request a kettle of hot water, please," she said into the tube.

"Which of you madwomen is speaking? For it sounds like no Jamaican bird!" Mr Hardwick's voice snapped faintly from the round mesh in the box the calling tube was attached to. Elle heard great machinery clank.

"This is Mrs Black speaking into the tube, Mr Hardwick," she said. "If you'll send me the ascension room, I would like to visit with you."

Elle found the chamber's descent both exhilarating and alarming. She'd properly shut the gate and door behind her, then turned to view the reception area through the glass door opposite. Once the reception area disappeared from view and all she could see was blackness, she decided to trust the rumbling cage and enjoy the ride.

"How interesting, to be in a moving box!" she marvelled, glad it was lit by an electrical light.

Seconds later, it slowed with great hisses of steam and revealed a sprawling basement space filled with slowly working machinery and lit by boiler fires and dim gaslights. It was hot and more humid than the Egyptian deserts of Elle's childhood. Giant gears and other parts were piled on the floor or hung from walls. Some machines looked in a state of repair, their pieces dismantled. When the ascension room came to full stop, Elle slid the door and gate aside. Mr Hardwick, dressed in his workman trousers, leather apron, and bearing a huge wrench in hand, lurched towards her.

"So this is what you do all through the day and night, Mr Hardwick?" Elle greeted above the rhythmic clank and clatter.

"It is indeed! And what were you doing before disturbing my toil within Sundark's organs and bowels?" he said. "Knitting?"

Coal tumbled down a chute. Mr Hardwick leaned the great wrench against a pillar, took up a shovel, opened the grate to a boiler's fire, and began feeding it.

"Even while knitting I am detecting, Mr Hardwick," Elle said as she came beside him. She removed the cloth covering the basket and showed him the contents within. The aroma of freshly baked steak pies rose.

"Would you share luncheon with me?" she said.

Mr Hardwick led her to a work area where a huge plan of the inner workings of Sundark was pinned. After clearing off a bench and wiping his hands, he bade her sit and joined her to partake of her offering.

"Welcome to the true Sundark!" he said, sweeping his hand as the other held his pie. "All the work of a madman, and I love it."

Elle, with her basket and pie in her lap, admired their noisy surroundings and then studied the hung plan. She noted the many large, red X's. She wondered where she and Mr Hardwick were located, for the machinery drawn on the plan seemed to go on and on in a sprawling fashion.

She then observed Mr Hardwick enjoying his pie with great bites and drinking his bottled beer and thought of how happy Faedra also looked when well fed and indulging in a brew. However, the pungent scent of his sweat-stained shirt ceased further comparisons with her wife. Valentin had been more like

Faedra in that even in exertion he smelled sweet, though Elle had known him to exert only in the bedroom. But he also barely ate, a strange disdainer of foods. The quality had displeased her, and such recollections of her dead husband made Elle frown.

"Josefina would bring me meals," Mr Hardwick said, apparently unaware of Elle's change in mood. "But I put a stop to that. It's too dangerous for her to come down here."

"Yet you allowed me to come, Mr Hardwick?" Elle said, preparing to take another bite of pie.

"Well, you're a witch, aren't you? Float things about like toy drums and tin horns? Frighten daimons with your black-rimmed eyes and blood-red hair? That's more than Josefina can do." He finished his meal and leaned back against the wall. He sighed, bottle in hand.

"Then why haven't you sent her away, Mr Hardwick?"

"She won't go," Mr Hardwick said grimly. "None of them will leave."

"But leave, they do, just not in the conventional manner."

Mr Hardwick's eyes widened briefly, and Elle saw his hard swallow.

"Josefina is very loyal," Elle added. "And concerned about you."

Mr Hardwick grunted.

"So have you learned anything yet, Mrs Black?" he said. "Now that you've seen that photographer's evidence? Much good it does us in explaining this damn business."

"I am still investigating, Mr Hardwick, but I have my thoughts."

"Ah. And am I to understand that you only seek remuneration for your fine detecting by my rewarding some widows and orphans? Are you by chance a very well-to-do widow? You certainly don't dress like one."

"Mr Hardwick, were my wife paid as much as her male peers, perhaps I could dress the part of 'well-to-do'!" Elle said hotly.

"Ha-ha-ha! You said 'wife' again."

"Mr Hardwick, if you must mention the matter of finances, why do you remain here?" Elle asked. "The Sundark clearly makes you no income, and it appears you are emptying the house of its contents."

"I didn't think we needed all those plants and books," he said.

"And the piano in the music room? The carpeting still retains the marks from where it sat."

"You do nose about, don't you? Fussy woman. I can take care of the creditors. I felt the need to . . . I'm not certain. Perhaps I'm preparing for a change."

"You intend to leave, then?" Elle said.

"Leave? Never."

Mr Hardwick rose and Elle watched him curiously.

"This . . . this! This is where my wife disappeared, Mrs Black," he said, raising his hands to indicate the house above them. The machines clanked. "My foolish heart waits for her return. Even if that return might be finding her bones, finally revealed in whatever earth or walls they've been hiding in."

He hung his head, seemingly pained by his own words.

"You may have to wait quite a time for that, Mr Hardwick," Elle said gently. "And perhaps . . . nothing more will happen. You could leave and have a new life with new people to care for."

"Ha! If I were entirely a different sort of man, yes, I would do that! How many times have I thought it? To be *done* with all of this? But how hard it is to just give up. Can you tell me that 'giving up' is not that, Mrs Black, an admittance of defeat? That it is something right to do, something more significant than I can yet know, to say such a 'good-bye'?"

"To say 'good-bye' is to give up something, Mr Hardwick," Elle said. "It always is."

"And there you have it," he said.

Mr Hardwick had little patience for entertaining guests. At conversation's end, he gave her his empty bottle, urged her to pack up the remains of her meal, and go. Once he shut the ascension room's gate behind her, he promised to show her a new aspect of the Sundark. He pushed the button.

Steam roiled. The room rose, and Elle watched until Mr Hardwick was no longer in her view. She watched more as she passed the first floor, the second, the third, and went beyond.

The chamber abruptly emerged into sunlight and air, birds erupting into the sky at the sudden appearance. As the room jerked to a halt within a wrought-iron pagoda, Elle slid back the door and gate, blinked, shaded her eyes, and looked out beyond the reception area's glass dome for the rooftop patio. Neglected wicker chairs and their small tables, worn by weather and sun, were scattered about. She stepped out.

Far across the roof patio a black Arabesque, domed tower stood with a blue door. Elle looked behind her and saw the Right Tower Josefina had climbed earlier. A trellis-like ladder led up to the dome beside the gold door. At another distance sat the third tower, highest amongst them with its dainty dome and slowly turning weathervane. The ladies' hands pointed intermittently at her. Elle went to the parapet and retrieved her dangling, compact spyglass on its chain.

She extended her glass and slowly surveyed all the land, looking for corpse roads. With the many trees and the property situated on a hill, it was hard to discern any faint paths. At the back of the house, she saw a barn and stables with Mr Arch tending to a horse and a little beyond that, the walled garden of the estate, thickly protected by a windbreak of trees. She trained her glass on what little of the garden's rows and fruit trees she could see over the wall. She wondered what was being grown, and why she'd yet to enjoy any better fruits and vegetables of that garden. She spotted Mr Willy slowly walking the ground with his head down, as if searching for something. He then stopped and began digging in a fertile row of tall, dark kale.

He lifted his shovel and quickly dumped dirt and an oddly shaped object into his barrow. It gave a brief flash in the sunlight before disappearing.

A *root?* Elle thought. But she knew that was not what she initially thought upon viewing.

Mr Willy threw an empty burlap bag over the barrow, then wheeled it beyond Elle's sight. She looked more at the spot he had dug at, spying nothing but huge kale leaves that quivered in the wind.

She lowered her glass and looked at her own hand. In the sunlight, her wedding band flashed, much like the twinkle she'd seen from the "root" in the shovelful of dirt.

CHAPTER FIVE

Elle descended the roof by entering the Left Tower and found Heric's former sanctum, the Blue Room, as unremarkable and empty as the Gold Room. There, the ceiling mural was painted gold with a black sun, and the trimming also was in gold. After poking about in the wing belonging to the servants and master, she sought out Josefina on the ground floor.

The young woman was labouring in her office in the reception area, reviewing the numbers in Mr Hardwick's accounting books. Her fingers clicked the black beads of an abacus. The postman arrived, marching in a military fashion, and gave Josefina a packet of mail with a genial salute before departing back down the hall for the outside and his wheel. Josefina handed Elle a letter from Faedra, which she accepted eagerly.

"You benefit from London marking post ten times a day," Josefina said in good humour. Elle put Faedra's letter in a dress pocket to enjoy later and saw Josefina's face grow annoyed at viewing the other letters in her hands.

"More bills," she sighed. She placed them with ones on her desk and turned to Elle, apparently noticing her guest's concern. "Oh, Mrs Black! No need for worrying. Mr Hardwick can take care of the expenses. Especially after all me help straightening his books and affairs these past months. Me only dislike bad business, and the Sundark is just that."

"Well, with the piano missing, the solarium empty—not to mention the state of the poor library—I'm afraid the impression is that expenses are a problem, Miss Dufish! How did Mr Hardwick manage before you came? Or did his wife's disappearance cause this decline? It seems all he does is remain below, to the neglect of all things."

"It be my understanding that Mrs Hardwick oversaw the hotel, Mrs Black. I can only do so much. I am a secretary, not a hotel manager," Josefina said with a shrug. She picked up a few papers and began shifting through them.

Elle moved about the office and took in the machinery diagrams pinned on the walls, the hanging pictures, the drafting items on Mr Hardwick's worktable, and the clutter on his desk. She saw no personal photographs. Elle assumed that any of his wife might be in his private chambers.

"A difficult position for you, Miss Dufish. As you've said, the Sundark is bad business and it can only grow worse from here on. Why remain?"

"Mr Hardwick needs me, of course," Josefina murmured. She cleared a spot on Mr Hardwick's desk, laid down the papers she'd put in order, and then positioned a pen and inkbottle by them.

Elle smiled. "He does indeed, or else I wouldn't be here. I do thank you for the arrangement that allows me to stay expense-free."

"Mrs Black, it be of no concern!" Josefina said. She gestured in dismissal. "We hardly have paying guests. Mr Lunt, for one, won't be paying now."

"Yet he must have a family to bill? A wife, certainly?" Elle said. "He did wear a ring."

"You noticed it too. No, he told us himself there be no-one any longer, of kin or spouse. He wore it out of memory."

"How sad. What will become of his things?"

Josefina shrugged. "I leave such matters to housekeeping, which would be Mrs Willy. Me not concern meself with a dead man's t'ings."

Elle nodded, then mentioned the garden, commenting on how its produce must help with food expenses. Josefina had an unkind opinion on that, saying that Mr Willy seemed far too busy with cultivating his prized manure pile to raise proper produce.

"He protects his own territory, Mrs Black, just like his wife does the kitchen," Josefina said to her in a low voice. "I haven't the keys to either, they've seen to that. But the barn you saw is unlocked. There are no animals. It was Heric Sundark's workshop. Once, it stored his devises, but no longer. We t'ink they be sold off by previous owners. All that remains are his water chamber and many restraints and chains, for his escapist demonstrations."

"Well, like Heric Sundark, I don't find locks a deterrent. I would like to take a look at the garden . . . if Mr Willy is sent away."

Josefina nodded. "I can send him on an errand, but tomorrow morning, he be departing for the day. With his wife, to see to an ailing aunt in Cheapside. They do so from time to time."

"Departing for Cheapside," Elle said thoughtfully. "I see. That is the opportunity I need. Thank you, Miss Dufish."

When Elle left Josefina, she heard female laughter from the parlour. Eden's voice rose, intent on telling a humorous tale. She and Fidela laughed more, and Elle smiled at the sound. Entering the drawing room on her way to the grand staircase, she saw Austin sitting in a chair behind his camera. He was positioned near the windows and therefore had a view of the entire room.

"Oh, Mr Washington! Back to work, I see?"

"I am, Mrs Black, for more evidence needs to be gathered," he said. He did not raise his hat to her, though his demeanour seemed improved since luncheon. "I feel that with my latest photograph, the Society of Psychical Research will surely send someone to the Sundark."

"Yes, they should come."

"Unless you solve all that is happening before they can. But your involvement can only intrigue them more." Elle watched his face brighten at the thought, looking more animated than she'd had occasion to see. "Mrs Black, may I impose on you for just a moment?" Austin rose from his chair.

Elle approached curiously and asked him what was the matter. In a contrite tone, he explained that he'd been sitting behind his camera for nearly three hours.

"Oh, Mr Washington, if you've need, certainly go!" she said.

"I would but . . . Miss Brunch is very curious about things."

"I will watch your camera," Elle reassured.

Austin thanked her and hastened away. He even touched the brim of his hat.

Elle heard the women giggle more in the parlour. She stood by Austin's camera and waited patiently.

She felt the room's air scatter away.

The room darkened before she could think to move. The hairs of her neck rose, and a chill entered her, sinking to the marrow. On the edges of her awareness, she spied someone.

The bare-chested man stepped beside her and walked past, hands in fists. She saw the hairs on his arms, the muscles of his shoulders, and the trim of his fringe beard. She tried to smell him and inhaled the scent of lightning. He appeared wet, as if just emerged from a swim in full trousers. His braces swung. His slick, black hair dripped. He continued walking towards the overmantle, the mirror above which remained shattered.

The tinkling sounds of a piano drifted in from the far-off music room. Elle grabbed her doll's mirror and turned around.

She watched the man through her mirror, with his broad, wet back and tense arms. He did not distort or lose cohesion as phantoms reflected in mirrors would. He looked as true to her as any human man. Then, in the remaining mirror fragment over the mantle she spotted his face.

His haunted gaze, deep and dark, was upon her reflection. But in the mantle's mirror, it was not her figure but Abigail Sundark's as she stood where Elle was, in her black dress and lace cape. Elle's own head wore Abigail's oily sausage curls.

Elle whirled and looked directly into the mantle's mirror. The black curls bounced. Abigail smiled from Elle's face.

"Quite a jest," Elle said, her voice a faint "pop" of sound that fell flat in the charged air. Yet in hearing her own words, she knew that she herself was still present in the room. She saw Abigail's face stare back at her, her gaze curious and cold. It began to melt. The man's face and form did the same. The last of his manifestation to fade were his sad eyes, watching her reflection in the mantle's mirror.

Austin walked in.

He looked around. "You were speaking to someone, Mrs Black?"

Elle resisted the urge to touch her own face. The air, no longer charged, smelled musty with the room's dust, and she could see the sunlight from the windows.

She took a breath. "It was more like I had spoken to 'something', Mr Washington."

My Beloved,

Have you enough feverfew tea, dear? With all the activity you're suddenly immersed in, I suspect you've had to apply your perturbationist abilities strenuously. I am proud that you declined the offer of soothing syrup and am in celebration with you for your resolve. You were a young girl in school when given your doses, and morphine is not an easy remedy to refuse.

Mr Lunt's disappearance gives me concern, but where bloodhounds may fail, I know you will find a way to recover him. I just hope he's in a condition that won't be gruesome. I am working on those tenant applications and the missing chicken as fast as

I can so that I may join you.

Now as to your first spouse: you say you might need spiritual assurance due to some lingering guilt, which may be why you have seen this "apparition" of Valentin. But dearest, how reassuring is it that you saw him helping a young lady, unknown to you, into a phaeton loaded with purchases from a dress shop, and himself smiling to that same woman? Then you said that both he and you saw the other, and at that recognition—for that was how you described it, a "recognition"—he boarded after the girl and the phaeton drove away. For such a "crisis apparition", he seems quite independent of action, fairly capable of emotion, and can keep his seat in a phaeton, unless that and the girl was a phantom occurrence as well.

I'm still of the notion that it was a living man you saw, one greatly resembling he who is now gone. And, Love, if your heart is so expanded by myself, then mine is ten times that for you and only what God could measure! You are my world. Hurry with this business or I shall fetch you.

In Eternal Love,
Faedra

After Elle read her wife's letter in her room and comforted herself with a chocolate, she resumed her detecting work. The approaching evening found her in the Third Tower that stood tallest to the rest, surveying the grounds with her spyglass. Josefina had given her the silver key and affirmed that it was the room, as the hotel pamphlet would have it, reputed to be the intimate retreat for Abigail . . . and her specially invited guests. Though Elle raised an eyebrow at the information, the implication was not lost to her.

"There are kinds of rituals performed that require sexual energies," she said. "It is not unheard of for magic practitioners to, well, copulate with those who would be most useful for such workings. In the interest of greater effectiveness."

Josefina had merely pursed her lips in response and shuffled her papers.

Elle looked down from the Third Tower and watched Mr Willy slowly sweep his garden with a hoe, searching through his rows, fermenting manure stacks (to warm the potatoes), and under the growing vegetables. He'd yet to dig anything up, and Elle was weary of observing him, but he was not planting or watering and she doubted he was hunting for pests. It had occurred to her to investigate the garden at night, but she didn't want to miss any clues, even with her police lantern to aid her. More could be seen in daylight, and whatever Mr Willy was up to, she rather doubted he would be able to resolve it by morning. She turned her spyglass's attention to another side of the property.

She'd identified one faint path at last, leading straight from a grove up to the house before fading away. Were she to continue the line of direction, it would run to her present tower. She assumed that if she found the two remaining corpse roads they would lead to the Blue and Gold Towers. She dropped her spyglass to take up her notebook.

"I wonder what you've done, Abigail Sundark. For I don't believe the mistress of these roads is pleased."

She drew a line to represent the corpse road she'd found.

"The shirtless man is Heric, your husband," Elle said thoughtfully. She remembered how Abigail's eyes studied her own reflection. "And you wondered what he saw."

She drew a very small circle to represent the tower she was in. She then observed the position of the other two towers from her windows and drew large circles to represent their domes. She traced a careful triangle connecting all three locations.

She looked at her diagram.

"Oh, come now!" Elle laughed, but she couldn't deny that the drawing had manifested into a simplistic female representation; the domes were breasts, the smallest tower was a certain anatomical aspect, especially considering the room's reputed purpose, and the sole corpse road line denoted the separation of legs. Shaking her head, she drew an oval above the domes and gave it hair and features like Faedra's.

She exited the third tower via a door to the rooftop and

traversed it for Abigail's Right Tower. Once she found the second corpse road, she travelled to the Left Tower. She was noting the position of the third road when the house began its rotation for the evening. Elle spotted Mr Willy as the Blue Room slowly spun. He'd abandoned his search of the garden and was walking to the house. Once movement ceased, Elle descended.

On the third floor, she inserted the gold key Josefina had lent her and turned it a full rotation in the blue door's lock when she stopped.

"Turning," she said. She pulled up her notebook and flipped through the pages until it opened to her map with Faedra's portrait.

Taking her pencil, she drew the road lines out further until they intersected within the house. Hekate's hidden crossroad lay at the heart of the triangle formed by the turning towers.

"And now we're locked in," Elle said.

Dinner was an uneasy affair, made more so by the weak ox tail soup, tough mutton cutlets, and old mashed turnips. But the grilled mushrooms had flavour, and Elle thought that a great forgiveness because she'd never known a mushroom to ever lack flavour. Mr Lunt's seat at the table was empty and Austin did not bother to fill the position. Mr Hardwick, just as he had been at breakfast, glowered in silence and brought a pall to the table. Josefina ignored her employer, Austin busied himself with his meal, and Eden, no longer in her Arabian dress, picked at her plate and made unhappy noises, apparently irritated. Yet by what, Elle did not know.

"Did you know," Austin suddenly announced, as he fetched bread from the basket, "that Mrs Black witnessed more apparitions today? Just like the ones I photographed."

"Indeed!" Fidela said. "Mr Washington told us of your experience in the drawing room, Mrs Black, well done!"

"Did you photograph these duppies as well, Mr Washington?"

Josefina asked.

"I did not. But one of the ghosts was Abigail Sundark, whom I've photographed before."

"Extraordinary," Fidela said in wonderment. "I've yet to meet Sundark's spirits. Have you, Miss Dufish?"

"I have, Miss Sweetwater, one too many times," Josefina said.

"And you, Miss Brunch?" Mr Hardwick interjected. The sudden sound of his voice startled Elle. "Have you witnessed what Mrs Black has seen?"

Eden tossed her fork down on her plate.

"The powers of Sundark do not speak to me in that manner," she said.

"Yet I would not call the Sundark's manifestations 'ghosts'," Elle said. All looked at her expectantly—except for Eden, who fussed with the caper sauce and made a small hill with her mashed turnips.

"If a ghost is a true spirit of a departed person, and perhaps had the working mind of that person, then . . . I must say that I've yet to encounter a true ghost."

"'A true ghost'?" Austin repeated. "By your definition, the new Secret Commission agent Artifice should be a true spirit. For she is surely a functioning individual."

"To clarify, Mr Washington, she is an artificial ghost," Fidela said, in the friendly, lecturing tone Elle associated with kind governesses. "I'm not entirely certain, but I think she may be more a construction imitating a ghost, rather than a true spirit.

"But now I am confused, Mrs Black," she continued, looking around Eden at Elle. "What did you witness today, if not spirits?"

"I call them phantoms, perhaps in the manner we might refer to 'visions'," Elle said. "For they are of mere matter, not always viscous as the Sundark's phantoms are, but still manifestations."

"The Sundark's spirits are beings without awareness, then?" Fidela asked, perplexed.

"I would not even name them 'beings', but more objects. For some are thick and some are thin," Elle said. "And I don't mean in type of body, but in substance. Like when dust is in a sunbeam.

Weak phantoms are such."

"We know that, Mrs Black, they are weak for trying to reach us from the Fourth Dimension!" Eden said. "And having no body any longer, this is why they float about and such."

"Yes, Miss Brunch, perhaps that is the reason, assuming they are people."

"Of course they're 'people', Mrs Black! Or once were, what else can they be?" Eden said.

As she spoke, the sauce bowl trembled.

Elle saw its motion and looked at Eden, who stared back indignantly.

"Mr Hardwick," Fidela pleasantly said. Elle watched those present turn their attention to him. No-one appeared to have noticed the sauce bowl's movement.

"What are your thoughts?" Fidela asked.

"I think you are all the flightiest of birds," Mr Hardwick said, his voice like a hammer. "For I've seen none of these things. Not one visitant."

Dessert was a baked arrowroot pudding, and Elle was relieved that it hadn't the acrid taste of being scorched before being put in the oven. Nothing else trembled on the table, though Elle kept an eye on Eden, and after Mr Hardwick's observation on ghosts, table conversation ceased. But when he rose for the nightly Sidereal Dome viewing, all rose with him to follow, wiping mouths a final time or taking last sips of water. Elle wondered, as they filed behind his lumbering form up the stairs: was this the state of "betwixt and between"?

It was as if Neville's absence had stolen their social abilities and left them somnambulists, fallen into rote, complacent with the habitual. Right then, no-one had thought or purpose to leave that dangerous house, not even Josefina, as she surreptitiously helped Mr Hardwick up the steps. Elle could not discern if this herd-like behaviour was complacency or more alarmingly, submissiveness.

If she were to abandon this ritual viewing and depart for her room, would that break the liminal state? She thought not, for she would still be inside the Sundark, locked within Hekate's crossroads.

However, Elle knew that she possessed one advantage over the other guests: Faedra. Her wife existed outside the house, a treasure greater than any sorceress's casting could lull her into forgetting. And were she to forget, Faedra would, without a doubt, come for her. She touched her chest where her bullet-punctured coin pendant was tucked away and entered the Sidereal Dome.

As they filed into the darkness, Elle saw the designs above, of winged beings, skeletons, crows, and lions eating suns, all appearing brighter than they had before.

"Black sun," Elle said as she gazed at the glowing design of the sun being eaten, recalling the ones she'd seen earlier, painted on the ceiling of each tower room.

"Yes, Mrs Black, the Black Sun illuminates," Fidela said from the darkness.

"I haven't the alchemic knowledge you possess, Miss Sweetwater," Elle admitted. "What does it illuminate?"

"The Black Sun reveals the dissolution of our bodies," Eden suddenly answered. Elle turned and started. Despite the dark she could see Eden's silver hair glow.

"It will blacken us into ash, our final transformation, so that we may leave behind our mortal flesh at last!" Eden said.

Eden lifted her gaze for the ceiling, and Elle did the same. The sun design, Elle thought, seemed bigger.

"We will be souls flying unfettered to Venus," she heard Eden's hushed voice say.

"Such a . . . violent manner in which to hasten to the firmament," Elle said

"Like Semele before Zeus," Fidela remarked. "But this, as Eden describes, is transformation, Mrs Black. It is not the promise of merely becoming a shade, whiling away eternity in the Elysian Fields. It is a true ascension."

"And a most dramatic, alchemic transformation," Elle said.

Eden sniffed. "If becoming our next form were a simple process, Mrs Black, we would have all already taken it." The music began, and the dome cracked open.

The floor beneath them moved, and Elle, after viewing the sky for a time while Eden shouted out constellations, turned her gaze to her companions.

Austin seemed dutifully attentive to watching the sky. Fidela, too, was pleasantly enjoying the sights above. But beneath the light of the stars and peeping moon, Eden glowed, a presence brighter than the rest.

What was in that arrowroot pudding? Elle thought.

"Here we are! We are at the crossroads of the pathways! Open your doors that we may leave!" Eden cried to the heavens.

Elle looked at Mr Hardwick. His upturned gaze searched above, eyes soft.

Here we are, indeed. We've a chthonic goddess, the ghost of a very cunning woman, the ghost of her man who could design anything, Elle thought, studying his face. *And a pagan wife, as you'd said, Mr Hardwick . . . somewhere.*

The rotation and music ended. Everyone applauded. Eden spun as the dome rumbled shut, and Elle wondered what the turning of the great Sidereal Dome had locked in with them, right then.

CHAPTER SIX

My Darling Fae',

The investigation continues apace. I've uncovered more about the uncanny owners and of a possible chthonic power, harnessed here. That power being (and please keep an open mind, dear) the goddess Hekate. Yet the manner of the harnessing— if I'm determining it properly— only brings up the question: Why was it done? And even more importantly: did something go awry?

As to the vanished guests, I'll not discard more mundane (and insidious) chicanery yet, but I'll also not ignore the evidence of the fantastic, despite what such awareness implies of greater questions of life.

I am no spell practitioner. A common conjurer knows more than I of ensorcellment and the possible bindings laid here. For I believe something of that sort was laid, intricately and deeply. Neither blessed water nor sea salt can easily be thrown upon this predicament.

And there's also the matter of the apparitions, like the near-naked man I told you of, and their intention.

For an intention needs a mind, but whose mind is manifesting all this, I still don't know. Unless these occurrences are mere echoes, and by that I mean a forty-year-old memory, decaying, yet amplified by the very power of this house set on crossroads.

They appear, Faedy, like memories dwelled overly long upon, and perhaps are now greatly embellished, as some experiences can become to we living souls. If there is purposeful intent, a communication originating from somewhere or someone rather than my witnessing moving, spectral photographs of a time past, why the telling of it? Until I learn more—if such further learning is necessary, for my purpose remains in discovering how the guests are taken—my thoughts can only be circular on the "ghosts" matter. This leads me somewhat to another thought about Valentin's phantom.

Darling, it is true that my phantom seemed quite independent of action, accompanied by a girl and a phaeton, and yes, we had that visual connection of recognition. Yet I will still persist in my belief that it was a psychic vision. A Doppelgänger experience may occur as such, one that is a playing out of an event past, for I knew my Valentin to be a right rogue, and as you know, my family was against the idea of he and I marrying. He was a philanderer and penniless. So it rather stands to reason that I witnessed him as he once was; he in the past and I, here, the veils of time somehow lifted.

I will not take this occurrence as harbinger or omen, for I was not afraid or even dismayed at seeing him. The phantom event played as any scene of our living streets would, with no sense of dread or foreboding at all.

And I cannot say that I was even glad at the sight of him. Perhaps I've need of words. Of or about what, I just don't know, for ridiculous words come to mind: "How are you? What are you doing here? How very angry I am at you!"

And with such surprising words come to my vulnerable mind, perhaps therein is where my elusive reassurance resides. Mediums have made their coin from such a need, and despite my talents, I am just as susceptible, it seems, to my heart's mysterious business.

But no matter those mysteries, YOU, my darling, my beautiful one, you are my Heart. No circle of Hell can compare to the suffering I can create for myself should I have to exist without you. Has Mrs Sphinx's mate returned from the stonemason? She is needed, for all

*this talk of Hekate has me desire that our two lionesses stand ready
to protect you. Hekate the tri-fold goddess was flanked by great cats.
Ours must see to you. I will come home very soon.*
  Your Devoted Wife,
  Eleanor

Early morning found Elle seated in the rocking chair on the
round porch beneath the witch's hat dome, knitting, when Mr
Willy and his wife drove their cart around the house and down the
drive. She continued to knit until the cart disappeared beneath
the trees for the black gates below. She rose, leaving her knitting
on her chair, and swiftly walked around the building.

She descended the slope behind the house, passed the stable
and barn where Mr Arch and a boy were tending to the yard, and
approached the walled garden. She saw the chain and padlock
on the gates.

"Faedy shall certainly congratulate herself for having me
practice on all those old locks she brought home," Elle muttered.
She retrieved her brass tool-holder on its chatelaine chain. The
slender brass box hid tools that were revealed by pushing small
levers. One was a buttonhook, another a knife, the third was a nail
file, and the fourth —

Elle used her thumb to push the lever up. A sturdy lockpick
emerged from the brass housing. She inserted it into the padlock,
positioned it, and in feeling the lock's tumblers, created an image
of them in her mind. She moved them with a thought.

The padlock released with a click. Elle caught the lock, pulled
out her pick, secured the tool away, and removed the gate's chain.
She pushed the gate open to enter Mr Willy's domain.

As far as English gardens went, it was a decent walled garden,
though Elle though it rather neglected, with its espaliered fruit
trees needing trimming and fallow rows lacking seedlings. Since
Mr Willy had no assistants, it was far too big a space for one man to
maintain, which explained the empty, dirty greenhouse, disused

boiler, and row of barren hotbeds with their glass set aside.

Elle shook her head at the sight, recalling how she toiled over the creation of her own modest hotbed, from which her beloved strawberries presently grew. She passed the pea stalks, cabbages, turnips, and potatoes and stepped directly for the rows of kale. She looked for the hole Mr Willy had dug.

Finding it, she put her hand in and turned the earth, seeing nothing that could be a clue. She went to look for his barrow.

She peered inside the forcing shed, with its empty pots meant for rhubarb, the potting shed, and the sturdy store for picked apples and pears, on whose shelves Elle only saw a few old and rotting specimens. Hanging from the store's outside wall were gardening tools, long and short. Elle spied barrow tracks in the earth, leading away to the locked back gate. To her, the padlock resembled the one she'd just unlocked. She applied her mind to tripping the tumblers.

In seconds, she was outside the garden, following the path that led into the woods. There, the trees and bushes thickened and birds twittered. Elle followed her nose to a clearing. The barrow stood next to a high stack of decaying straw, cuttings, and other rotting greens mixed with horse droppings. It towered above her. A ridge sloped above where Mr Willy might stand as he worked the top of the pile. A pitchfork stood beside the mass, at the ready for turning the fermenting heap to keep its heat from becoming a smoulder. Six feet away, Elle spotted a pit. She went to peer into it.

A *pit kiln?* she thought. It smelt of fire, and was a simple, deep rectangular hole, its battered metal lid set aside. But as Elle knelt to look closer she saw little ash and no bits of pottery in the raked earth. She hadn't seen any smoke from the woods while dallying in the towers yesterday.

She searched for a sturdy stick. Finding one as stout as a walking stick and as long as her arm, she picked it up and approached the manure pile.

"Very odd of a gardener to not store his pitchfork properly," Elle said. "Which means you know exactly where it is, Mr Willy, and therefore must spend far too much time out here."

She stabbed the pile in the middle, poking for ash. She pondered what Mr Willy could be burning to add to his prized manure heap. When she pulled her stick away, a man's hand fell out.

Elle reeled, bile rising. Neville Lunt's soiled but still bright-blue kerchief dangled from the hole she made. The stiff, grey hand on the ground bore the indentation on the third finger of where a tight, gold ring used to be.

"*Craaaw craaaw!*" A carrion crow said above her.

Elle looked at the black bird and breathed deeply. Obviously, what was lying at her feet was no gnarled root. She thought to check if Mr Lunt's hand was drained or still had blood—or was cut clean, or torn, or so forth, in case such observations gave further clues, but she wasn't yet up to the task.

She heard a twig snap. She raised her stick in alarm.

Mr Willy stood before her, his eyes wide. He grabbed his pitchfork and Elle heard the carrion crow flap away.

With a great heave, she brought her stick down on Mr Willy's head.

He blocked it with his arm. She let go of the stick and stepped back, suspending it with her mind. She mentally swung it and struck Mr Willy again.

"*What?*" he shouted.

She brought the stick down on his arms, his hands, and then swung it directly into his face. He dropped his pitchfork, and Elle, with great effort, caught it with her mind and levitated it before Mr Willy, prongs aimed at his body.

"No! No!" he cried, and ran back to the garden's gate. Elle dropped the stick and pitchfork. She grabbed the barrow with her mind and sent it rattling down the path and into Mr Willy's backside. With a cry, he fell, and then scrambled for his feet for the garden. Elle ran after him. She mentally rammed Mr Willy with the barrow until he was forced to run for the store and take refuge. She sent the barrow hurtling into the shutting door with a resounding bang. She picked up a shovel and jammed it up against the doorknob.

"Come out, and I will *surely* end you, Mr Willy," Elle threatened in the most awful voice possible. Then she picked up her skirts and ran out of the garden for Mr Arch, her chatelaine jangling.

Elle's plan of searching Mr Willy's garden and incriminating the Willys for the petty theft she suspected them of was simple. She'd instructed Josefina the previous night to have the police accost the Willys before they crossed the Thames for Cheapside. The police had waited farther down the road as asked, but the Willys never arrived. Mr Willy's wagon had lost a wheel, and since they'd barely made distance from Sundark, he hurried back on foot.

Seeing his garden gate unlocked and ajar prompted him to investigate and thus discover Elle. The police, consisting of two constables, rode back and found Mrs Willy waiting patiently in the broken wagon with a carpetbag filled with Mr Lunt's belongings.

Mr Arch and his boy kept Mr Willy trapped in his store until two police inspectors with more constables arrived. The barn became the convenient place for the inspectors to interrogate the Willys and to organise a thorough search of the manure pile and surrounding area. Elle was allowed to be present in the barn and thus learned that the turning of the pile had uncovered more of Mr Lunt and the ash and smashed bones that might have been Mr Chipperings. It appeared that Mr Willy hadn't time to burn and pulverise Neville's remains before his wife wanted to sell the belongings.

Elle held her can of feverfew tea and sipped it as she looked at the barn's walls, hung with all manner of manacles and chains, former escapist tools of Heric Sundark. Mr Willy cringed in his chair as she passed, his wife beside him eying Elle's chatelaine.

The glass-and-iron contraption that had been Heric's water escape tank stood in the middle of the barn, apparently too heavy for transport by collectors or fellow illusionists. While Elle studied it, imagining an immersed and chained Heric Sundark within, Mr Hardwick stood before his seated employees, leaned on Josefina, and glowered.

"I tell you, we've done no wrong!" Mrs Willy protested.

"Stolen goods, Mrs Willy," one police inspector said simply. He was a solemn-faced and terse fellow. He held the carpetbag, some of its contents laid on the table. He'd arranged a few of Mr Lunt's tin samples and personal jewellery out for the police photographer.

"We've the responsibility of sorting the belongings of the vanished guests. We were only delivering them to the bereaved," Mrs Willy said.

"Mr Lunt was alone in the world, Mrs Willy. By the 'bereaved', do you mean the second-hand dealers in Cheapside?" Elle said, turning. "The goldsmiths would find Mr Lunt's wedding band of interest."

Mrs Willy shut her mouth tightly, but her gaze strayed again to Elle's chatelaine and eyed the dangling brass tools.

"To the wagon with her," the police inspector said with a curt gesture. "She'll only make her husband's fate worse."

"Don't you tell them anything they're wanting to hear!" Mrs Willy cried to her husband as two constables led her away. "We've done no wrong!"

Elle looked at Mr Willy as the second police inspector, a young handsome man with a fixed smile, bent over him. Mr Willy sat, his head hung, and rubbed his hands fretfully.

"Now, unlike that harridan of a wife, you're not proud enough to send yourself to the gallows. Isn't that right, Mr Willy?" the inspector said in a friendly manner. "Just tell us how this all came to be. An explanation might see you in prison, instead."

"I can't explain it, that's the problem, it can't be explained!" Mr Willy said. He raised his head to look ahead, and then ducked it again.

When Elle followed Mr Willy's line of sight, she saw Mr Hardwick, his gaze thunderous.

"Mr Willy, much of Mr Lunt's been dug out of your manure pile and pieced together by the local doctor," the inspector said. "I think we can explain that much. You and the wife killed the guests for their valuables."

"No, no! It's not that way at all!" Mr Willy said. "We've done nothing but watch!"

"Watch?" the inspector said. "Who else is involved that you must watch?"

Mr Willy pointed in the direction of the Sundark, his finger shaking.

"The house!" he cried. "It's the house that wants 'em! The house that eats 'em!"

"Who in the house, Mr Willy?" Elle asked sharply.

Mr Willy stared imploringly at Mr Hardwick.

"It's the *house*, sir. After the house eats 'em, they show up in the garden. Like they'd been chewed and spit. I'd find the bits of 'orror, come up in the rows. In the *garden*, sir! We don't know why, we don't know *how*. We couldn't tell anyone because you'd all suspect it was us what done it. But we didn't. We only picked up the pieces."

Mr Hardwick rushed at Mr Willy. He hauled him up, the chair falling with a bang. He shook Mr Willy in the air.

"Where is my *wife*?" Mr Hardwick roared.

It took several constables and the inspectors to force Mr Hardwick to put Mr Willy down. Mr Willy collapsed on the barn floor.

"She never appeared! Not one bit of her!" he cried.

He covered his face with his hands.

"I swear it," he sobbed. "I swear."

After Mr Willy's confession, Mr Hardwick stormed out of the barn and made his laborious way up to the house. Josefina

nearly followed, then shook her head. She and Elle departed as
the inspectors conversed privately. Mr Willy sat on the floor and
sobbed.

"Mrs Black, you asked who it be in the house that is causing
this," Josefina said.

"Yes, Miss Dufish. If only to make Mr Willy clarify what he
meant."

"Well! Them fire duppies," Josefina snorted as they stood in the
sunlight. "Now I be thinking they're a conjure, like the voodoo
men do. The Willys' rooms should be searched for trickery!"

Elle looked over Josefina's shoulder and saw Mr Arch, lingering
by the stable with neighbour folk and children surrounding him.
All stared curiously in Elle and Josefina's direction and held
hushed conversations.

"Perhaps. But if it is as Mr Willy says, I wonder why he and his
wife didn't leave, if the house itself was murdering its occupants,"
Elle said.

"That be the t'ing, Mrs Black! He can blame a haunted house,
for it cannot speak back! The Willys are our best suspects for the
vanishings."

"Indeed, though I believe greed can make anyone foolish, until
they're blind to the danger for themselves. But your neighbours
are now very relieved," Elle said, nodding in the direction of Mr
Arch's group.

"I should see to them. It be nearing luncheon, and I'm certain
those hampers the ladies be bearing are for picnics," Josefina said,
smiling.

"As this is now a murder investigation, I doubt they may enter
the Sundark, but perhaps the inspectors will allow them to picnic
before the front of the house," Elle said. Josefina expressed her
intent to speak to an inspector and left to do so.

Elle turned her attention away from the stable and looked
towards the walled garden. Constables had their heads down,
slowly sweeping the grounds outside and inside the walls with
canes and sticks. She glanced up at the house.

The Sundark's many art glass windows gleamed. The glass of

the solarium twinkled in the midday sun, its interior woefully
barren of plants. Faded curtains obscured rooms that Elle knew
held no furnishings. Yet she thought the house, rather than
looking neglected and empty, remained as solid and inviolate
a presence as ever, its vitality undiminished by the lugubrious
happenstance of murders.

Elle felt someone walk by and saw it was the younger inspector,
his notebook and pencil in hand.

"Inspector," Elle addressed him. She walked with him as he
approached the garden's gates. "Mr Willy was searching in his
garden most all of yesterday, and I don't believe he found what
he'd sought."

"That might be the last piece of Mr Lunt, Mrs Black," the
inspector said. He stopped at the entrance. "The doctor has the
corpse all assembled, except his left foot is missing."

A constable poking in an apple tree suddenly gave a shout.
They turned in time to witness Mr Lunt's left foot falling and
striking the constable on the helmet. It still wore a shoe.

"Oh! There it is," the inspector said.

Once the foot was delivered to the doctor, the constables
resumed their search, though Elle wondered whatever for,
except perhaps to discover further gruesome evidence of earlier
disappearances. Elle asked the inspector what he thought of a
murderer who would fling the body parts about in his garden
and then go looking for them again, but he merely waved her
questions away.

"Mrs Black, we must consider accomplices," he said.

"And consider also the accusation made against the house and
the evidence of preternatural activity, which I have personally
witnessed. I believe we should all vacate and you may question us
at another location."

"Nonsense," the second inspector said as he approached them.
His terse manner was made more brusque by what Elle suspected
was a short temper. "You are all to remain in the house. No-one
is to leave, and a man will be on duty outside to make certain of
that."

"Even myself, who was summoned here to assess the presence of supernatural activity and investigate the disappearances?" Elle said incredulously.

"Mrs Black, if you would return to the house," the inspector said curtly. He brushed by her and quickly made his way up the slope to the Sundark. He disappeared through the scullery entrance, followed by a constable.

The younger inspector then smiled and politely urged Elle towards the house.

Elle returned as bidden and entered the folding French doors of the back veranda in ill temper. She crossed the ballroom proper, her steps echoing on the floorboards, and exited into the reception area. Here she saw Austin, camera and folded tripod under an arm, poised as if to flee. He was looking in the direction of the dining room. He then straightened at her presence.

"When I'd said I hoped you'd solve this business, I didn't mean for you to do so in this manner," Austin declared.

"Mr Washington?" Elle said in surprise.

"Thanks to you, the disappearances are now blamed on common murderers! Constables are everywhere, looking for evidence of trickery. An inspector demands answers from we guests as if we, too, could be a part of some elaborate, bizarre banditry! Such supposition invalidates my hard-won photo of Mr Lunt. Miss Dufish presently thinks the blue spectres I've captured are really tricks with phosphorescence and muslin!"

"Mr Washington, if it would comfort you, I assure you that phantoms *are* present in this house."

"Yes, Mrs Black, but your word holds no weight in convincing the Society of Psychical Research. Already Miss Dufish has forgotten the many supernatural occurrences that had plagued us these past months. I will not accept that the Willys and their imaginary accomplices haunted us so successfully by mere chicanery. And to insist on normalcy after all that has happened? That is no answer!"

"Yet 'normalcy' is what Miss Dufish wishes for, Mr Washington," Elle gently said. "One man's desire for adventure or answers is often one woman's desire for stability and peace."

Austin quieted. Elle continued.

"The police will exhaust their investigation, very soon, and then we may leave."

"Leave? That, I can't do, not while—well, I just can't."

Elle looked at Austin curiously. He shifted his tripod and avoided her gaze.

Well, Elle thought. *I can guess why, considering how many tintypes you have of her, Mr Washington.*

"It appears there won't be any luncheon since you had Mrs Willy taken away," he then said.

"Mr Washington, several neighbours have come calling in curiosity now that Mr Lunt has been found. Perhaps they'll share the contents of their picnic hampers with you."

To her surprise, Austin flinched.

"I've seen the picnickers," he said. "If you'll excuse me."

Elle, exasperated, watched him hurry away. He nearly ran down the hall for the drawing room.

"That man," she said under her breath.

She sighed and pulled up her notebook on its chain. She flipped to her drawing of Faedra's portrait and the crossed corpse roads. All three spirit paths, she believed, intersected—

She stepped towards the centre of the reception area.

"Picnickers in front, searching policemen in back, and here we are, scurrying about inside of you," Elle announced as she looked above at the glass dome with its black sun. Her voice echoed.

"Now what have you to say to we mere mice within your walls?" she said. "Such incredible accusations have been made against you."

She heard a rumble. The dome above began to slowly rotate, and Elle realised that the midday turning of the Sundark was commencing. Even within the reception area, she could hear the faint voices of excited children exclaiming outside.

Yet this is no place for children, Elle thought.

Then she felt a great chill enter her bones, as if the very spot she stood on were made of ice.

She lowered her gaze and saw Abigail Sundark standing before her.

The chamber around them began to spin, like a merry-go-round, though Elle knew that was not possible. She stared into Abigail's bright, bold eyes, saw her oiled curls and the delicate black lace around her white shoulders. Abigail raised a finger to her lips, and slowly pointed above.

Elle tore her gaze away and looked up.

On the third story open-air corridor, she saw Abigail arguing with the old woman in the severe bonnet, Heric's aunt. Abigail gesticulated wildly. The aunt stepped back and the railing broke. As she tottered, Abigail's face was a mixture of horror and realisation. The old woman fell through and down.

"No!" Elle cried, and tried to catch her with her mind. She heard a horrendous crack as she struck the floor.

The scene changed. Elle found herself looking above again. Abigail repeated her wild gestures, her mouth forming the same words. The girl standing before her was Minona Hodges. Minona stepped back like one woodenly rehearsing the part of a play, fell through the railing and down towards Elle.

Elle stretched her arms out and saw the passive lifelessness of Minona's face.

Once more, the scene changed, and Elle looked above again. This time a woman in modern clothing, her bodice and skirts emerald-green, stood before Abigail. She wore a necklace of moonstones and her long red hair was loose. She stepped back in the same manner as Minona Hodges. The railing broke behind her.

"Stop," Elle said.

The reception area was empty. She heard people arguing in the dining room, and wondered if she were trapped within the manifestation still. She breathed, heart hammering.

The registry book, pen, and the chairs of the reception area, held aloft by her mind's agitation, fell with loud bangs to the floor.

"You *harpy*," Elle said through clenched teeth.

She heard swift footsteps from the dining room. Eden hurried into the reception area, dressed in her white silk robe, Arabian bloomers, and turban. The young inspector and Fidela, holding her HEKATE book to her breast, pursued her. Eden raised an accusing finger at Elle.

"You!" Eden said.

"Oh, heavens," Elle said.

"How *dare* you seek to obstruct the sidereal workings of this sacred locus!" Eden said, shaking her fists at her. "Mr Lunt's true self resides in the great firmament. His body is but an empty vessel now, which you've somehow retrieved and desecrated. And why not, if not to validate your position as a petty, little psychic sleuthhound?"

"Miss Brunch!" Elle said, shocked.

"Eden," Fidela said in dismay.

"Miss Brunch," the inspector said. "You're saying that Mr Lunt, in your psychic opinion, was borne away by these apparitions after all?"

"Yes! Yes! How many times must it be said?" Eden hotly stated. She stamped her foot.

The angry sound echoed in the reception area, and Elle saw all the fallen chairs around them begin to tremble.

"Who are the blue apparitions, then, Miss Brunch?" Elle asked, eying the quivering chairs. She raised a placating hand. "Why did they take Mr Lunt away?"

"How very dense you are, for all your professed abilities in 'seeing' them!" Eden said. "They are the fallen, taken before their time, and are therefore ghosts of great power. In ancient times these were warriors, gladiators, the *murdered*. Summoned, these servants of the liminal goddess can do a great many things, but most of all, escort us in the journey home!" Eden pointed to the dome above. "To Venus!"

"Yes. As you've explained, which occurs through the alchemic process," Elle said.

"Yes! This is the *true* working of the Sundark, Mrs Black. And once you *believe*," Eden said, "then you are received!"

"Yet did Mr Lunt believe?" Elle said.

The chairs around them suddenly clattered. Eden turned on her heel and stormed away. The inspector looked about for the cause of the noise, shook his head, and followed. Elle stayed Fidela with a hand.

"Miss Sweetwater, I do believe Eden, I know that those who died too soon are somehow fuel for this house. But I don't believe the purposing of this locus was of lofty intent but more of malevolence. Just look at the towers and domes around us, turning, always turning, like keys to lock us in!"

"Keys which lock us in?" Fidela repeated softly, baffled. "Oh, no . . . no, Mrs Black! The ritual turning is the whir of the strophalos, the life-generating wheel of Hekate. The towers are magic wheels!"

Elle looked at her in confusion. Fidela took her woven silk bookmarker from her HEKATE book, flipped the pages to a spot, and marked it.

"And such wheels may be used to summon the Tri-fold One, Mrs Black. And . . . more. Here," Fidela said. She pressed the HEKATE book in Elle's hands and hurried away in the direction Eden and the inspector had disappeared.

Elle held the book in befuddlement. She turned and saw Josefina at the reception area's entrance, bearing two cloth-covered baskets. Josefina returned her gaze with a quizzical expression.

"There's been far too much activity in this area for my liking," Elle said. "Though I am to blame for at least one occurrence."

"Mrs Black, you be talking like a medium," Josefina said teasingly. She approached and showed Elle the contents of one of the baskets. Elle saw cold ham, cheese, bread, and apples. "The inspectors will not let our neighbours into the hotel, but they be celebrating the arrest of the Willys with us. In generosity, they've provided luncheon."

"Excellent, Miss Dufish, for there is a matter I would have attended to sooner had I not been delayed by our fellow Sundark inmates." Elle liberated the smaller of the baskets from a surprised Josefina and walked to the gate of the ascension chamber.

She pulled down the speaking tube from the wall.

"Mr Hardwick," Elle called. "I must speak with you, at once."

After a moment's pause, Elle heard the engine start that would send the ascension room above. She sighed as she watched the counterweight drop and the cables swiftly run.

When Elle emerged from the ascension chamber, she hesitated, uncertain if she was in the right place. The great space seemed more congested with machinery than before, with valves, pipes, snaking cables, and immense, turning cogs. Yet there were piles of parts sitting in oily spots on the floor, waiting to be reinstalled or to be discarded. She finally spied Mr Hardwick on the same bench they'd shared luncheon on, his great diagram with its red X's rent and tossed in a crumpled heap to the ground. Mr Hardwick sat, slumped, surrounded by giant wrenches and pliers, his broad brow darkened.

Elle made her way to the bench, hefted a very large wrench aside, and sat by him.

After a while, she spoke.

"Moonstones," she said.

Mr Hardwick turned and looked at her.

"Seems very appropriate. Moonstones for witches," she said.

"How do you know this?" Mr Hardwick's voice was low and harsh.

"I only guessed," Elle said.

Mr Hardwick turned and gazed sightlessly at the floor.

"We had an argument that day," he said softly. "A foolish one. She only wanted me to join her in the Sidereal Dome. I told her I could join her in that silly place anytime. Right then I had been busy. With the engines.

"She accused me of loving the machines more, and left. She took the ascension chamber with her.

"She never sent it back down. Finally, I climbed the stairs. I looked in the Dome. . . I looked everywhere. No-one had seen where she'd gone."

Elle grasped his hand. She held it firmly. Mr Hardwick closed his eyes.

Eventually, after a few sombre reflections on Valentin and Mrs Hardwick, Elle felt hungry and let go. She delicately wiped engine grease off her fingers, put together a ham, mustard, and cheese sandwich, and commenced eating.

"Isn't that my lunch?" Mr Hardwick said.

Elle swallowed and dabbed her mouth. "Well, you may have some of it, Mr Hardwick, but if you don't take your share, I will eat all of the lemon cake."

He took the basket from her and helped himself to the contents.

Elle ate and mused on wakes and how they comforted the living. Despite Mr Hardwick's renewed grief, food seemed to soothe his hurt and give him some temporary peace. Elle looked around at the jumbled machinery, thinking them noisier than before, and fanned herself with the HEKATE book. If the first level of hell had a modern aspect, it might look like this, she thought.

"You continue to keep the Sundark in splendid working order," she said.

"Silly woman! All of that is more a splendid mess," he said, gesturing at the machinery. "Did the midday turning of the house occur?"

"It did, without fail."

Mr Hardwick growled and stuffed cake in his mouth.

"Mr Hardwick, I don't believe the disappearances will end, do you?" He scowled. "I will take that as affirmation. You must convince the inspectors to let us leave the Sundark."

"Of course, of course! I've been wanting you all to leave!" he said. "But I must remain."

"Mr Hardwick, you no longer need to remain. Your wife will never return."

He stared at her as if she'd spoken Egyptian.

"In all certainty, trust my word, she is gone," Elle said. "Perhaps to Venus, and no, she cannot come back for you nor send you any sort of sign. I don't know what fantasy you are entertaining, but if you still insist on remaining, Josefina will remain. Then Mr Washington will refuse to depart and I cannot, in good conscience, leave a client endangered. Therefore none of us will leave!"

"Josefina will leave with you, and I'll make certain of it! I'll do what I should have done months ago. I'll dismiss her."

"Really," Elle said sceptically.

"You should return to your knitting," he tersely said.

Elle took the basket, rose, and left his side.

As she made her way to the ascension chamber, she heard him remark above the din of the machines.

"You are lucky, Mrs Black. At least you know that your husband is well and truly dead!"

Elle paused, recalling the manifestation in the reception area.

"But I certainly don't trust the source of that particular vision," she muttered beneath her breath. She turned to look at him.

"I can't explain how I know, but I know your wife is dead," she said. "She is as dead as my husband buried under the ground."

"I appreciate that you are most shockingly forthright, but let me query further." Mr Hardwick rose and lurched forwards. His eyes were fierce like lit fires. "You *saw* her. Is that right, Mrs Black? With your witch's eyes. You have seen my wife."

"Mr Hardwick, I saw an aspect of your wife."

"Very well. Then tell me this: if you were to know that some aspect of he who is gone was somehow still here, *somewhere* — as long as that awful possibility has a chance of being true, wouldn't you believe then, that your husband were *truly* still here?"

"No, Mr Hardwick, I would not believe such an aspect were truly him. He is gone."

"And that's where we differ. Good day, Mrs Black."

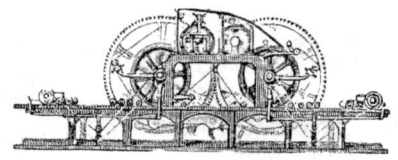

CHAPTER SEVEN

By evening, all police and curious visitors had departed, headed for homes where dinner awaited. Even the journalists and their illustrators and photographers abandoned their queries, especially when attempts to enter the Sundark were foiled by the large constable left behind to guard the residents within. Elle, in her room, watched the last journalist leave by hansom cab for the town's hotel and wished that all within the Sundark were doing the same.

She enjoyed another letter from Faedra, one that assured her the twin of Mrs Sphinx had returned home and was back at her station, guarding their entrance. Faedra also wrote all manner of sweet, loving words which poured into Elle's needy eyes and reassured her that no matter how many times the spectre of Valentin should show itself, her love and utter trust in Elle remained true. Feeling ridiculously buoyed, like a child promised ten balloons when the one had popped, Elle tucked the scented letter into her bodice and hugged it.

She soon descended and found Josefina in the kitchen by following the scent of chicken being boiled. Never one to be idle in a kitchen, she found a clean apron to don and offered her aid. In good humour, Josefina promptly assigned her the task of onion-chopping. Elle thought Josefina in very good spirits, all the more uplifted by being able to meet and converse with the Sundark's local folk and enjoy the support of the community. She also did not look like a secretary, in Elle's estimation, who'd just learned she was dismissed from her position.

"What is it that we're making?" Elle asked as she sniffled over her pile of chopped onions. Josefina tilted the huge pot she was tending on the hot stove so Elle could see. "Oh, you've seared that lovely piece of ham hock beautifully! Then you'll be needing these."

Elle walked her board of chopped onions over to Josefina, who was dumping in crushed garlic and chopped green peppers.

"This will be Hoppin' John, Mrs Black," Josefina said, smiling. She took Elle's onions and slid them into the pot. The contents loudly sizzled. "It will have rice and black-eyed peas. Mr Washington's been hoarding a small sack of such peas, sent by his mother. The moment Mrs Willy was escorted from the kitchen, me be giving those peas the quick boil and soak!"

"Ham, rice, black-eyed peas! Oh, how very American!" Elle exclaimed.

"If Mr Washington had cornmeal, we be making cornbread too." Josefina grinned. She raised the lid on the boiling chicken with a blackened wooden spoon. Austin suddenly poked his head into the kitchen, saw both women, and nearly raised his hat. As if remembering his usual lack of manners, he quickly withdrew.

"That man," Josefina muttered, rolling her eyes.

Elle returned to her station, where freshly washed celery and tomatoes awaited her knife. Josefina pulled the tie of a leather folder with the gold initials JMD, unfolded it, and revealed labelled pouches holding small metal containers of spices. Elle watched her measure out thyme and cayenne, then black peppercorns for grinding. She also pulled out a dried bay leaf and tossed it into the pot.

"Seeing Mr Washington just now reminded me of something he'd mentioned. Apparently you're presently of the notion that all the phantom occurrences are an elaborate sham," Elle said as she quickly chopped. "Like the bare-chested man in the hallway, and such."

"I be thinking those were magic lantern shows," Josefina declared.

"Hmm. Yet today, I believe I may've met what would be considered a true ghost," Elle said.

Josefina turned to her in astonishment, pestle in hand. "Mr Lunt?" she asked fearfully.

"Oh no. It was Mrs Sundark. She looked at me directly, as if truly, I was the subject of her gaze. And she was intelligent of eye. Yet I wonder." Elle paused and pondered. "Ghost, or still a magic lantern projection of a mind? For the entirety of what she wanted me to see was indeed a concoction from her . . . or something's imagination."

"Mrs Black," Josefina said patiently. "Perhaps you should tell me the story. But after you be helping me add the stock and peas."

Once the large pot was simmering with peas, spices, and freshly ground seasonings, filling the air with a warm and delicious fragrance, they took seats at the kitchen table and Elle related her latest supernatural encounter.

"The first vision with Heric's aunt must be true," Elle finally said. "But the ones after were symbolic; a brief way to relay, however cruelly, a simple message to me. Abigail made a mistake, but it was one made right upon the crossroads she had wanted to control. Further deaths fuelled whatever sorcery she had casted there. If Miss Sweetwater is correct, then the turning of the Sundark is the act of turning 'magic wheels', and in this way a chthonic entity has been summoned by the power of such deaths and unleashed here."

"Me not liking this story," Josefina said.

"Do not worry," Elle said, and laid a hand on her friend's arm. "I have spoken to the inspectors. Come morning there will be a change. A change that will include everyone."

"Mrs Black, I be very glad I asked you here," Josefina said, smiling.

"I am happy to help, but oh! I can't wait to return

to Faedra," Elle said. She rose to clear her neglected station and wipe it clean. Josefina rose as well to look within the simmering pot and set the rice, tomatoes, and celery at the ready.

"Mrs Black, how did you and Mrs White-Black first meet?" Josefina asked curiously.

"Why, we were in school together, Miss Dufish," Elle said. "I was ten, she was fourteen. She had come from abroad, as her mother was British but her father was American. Because of her manners and speech, the other girls chose to be rude to her straightaway! They called her terrible names."

"Oh, I know what they be saying. Did they call her, 'Fraida'?" Josefina said. She grinned as she stirred.

"Oh, Miss Dufish!" Elle said.

"That be easy to guess. And you stood by her 'gainst the rude girls?"

"I wish I could say I did. She punched them all so swiftly for their cruelty. And because of her actions, she was confined and given nothing to eat. The school had her thus for three days. Each night I saved part of my bread and went in secret to her confinement to give it to her."

"You loved each other then?"

"Oh, we loved as schoolgirls do. I adored Faedy. She was so beautiful, and fearless, and took no 'guff' from anyone! It wasn't long before she was the pride of the school, excelling in academics and athletics. But once of age, she left England to rejoin her father, and I. . . I eventually met my husband."

"The one who was shot, Mrs Black?"

"Yes, that's correct, Miss Dufish. In a duel. Where he also killed my brother."

Elle returned to the table and resumed her seat. Josefina joined her after adding the remaining ingredients to her Hoppin' John. Elle reached into her bodice and pulled out her coin pendant with the bullet hole.

"Here. This is a replica of the penny that was in Valentin's breast pocket when he was shot. I found it when I tried to staunch his bleeding. I held it even as he was taken away from me.

But when I went mad it was lost, and it was something I could not stop asking for."

"And this is a replica, Mrs Black?" Josefina said curiously.

"Yes." She unclasped the necklace and gave Josefina the coin to examine. "Faedra returned to England and came to look for me, you see. Imagine her surprise finding me mad, freshly widowed, and in an asylum. She heard my ranting for the coin. She went out every day with her pistol to shoot pennies until she thought the hole was just right. Then she gave it to me. Finally, I had my penny, my precious bit of Valentin, and once placated, my raving ended. I cannot say that true sanity was what cleared my eyes, but I could finally recognise her. My Faedy."

Josefina smiled warmly and returned the pendant to Elle.

"If only some could love again as you do," she said with a wistful sigh. "Hoppin' John be a food of good fortune. I be celebrating your happiness with you."

Elle helped Josefina serve the table, bringing out bread, Hoppin' John, braised parsnips, and a simple Mulligatawny soup, which Elle prepared thanks to the curry powder in Josefina's spice kit. The guests—Eden and the usually gruff Mr Hardwick included—were surprisingly well behaved and at ease. Elle thought perhaps Mr Hardwick's decision to dismiss Josefina made him desire to soothe the pending news with geniality. And though Elle regretted her last parting remark to Eden in the reception area and wished to make amends, the opportunity to do so passed too soon and Eden's serene bearing dissuaded Elle from selfishly disturbing such equilibrium.

While Eden in her turban and silks ate with the regal attitude of a sultana, Austin tackled his plate with vigour and nodded his approval to Josefina. Like Mr Hardwick, he seemed determined to be pleasant, and Josefina, maintaining the reserve and decorum of a proper lady, rather enjoyed the felicitations of the two men on either side of her.

But when Elle looked around Eden to ask Fidela if she found the Hoppin' John enjoyable, she thought the spinster had a distracted air.

"Oh, Mrs Black and Miss Dufish! It's certainly a most substantial dish, with such texture and flavours for the palate," Fidela said. Her enthusiastic words did not seem to match the concern Elle could see in her eyes.

"I enjoy it as much as the dishes of India," Fidela added.

"The green peppers do remind one of such heat in Indian cuisine," Elle said. "As does the curry in the Mulligatawny soup."

"Mrs Black, did you manage to do more reading?" Fidela asked. "From the book I lent you."

Elle saw Eden pause in her meal, and though she looked at neither woman, Elle felt Eden was making her awareness of their conversation known.

"Oh! Miss Sweetwater. I have been busy, but I will read it tonight," Elle said.

"Oh! Splendid. Splendid," Fidela said, and quickly returned her attention to her plate.

Dessert was a fluffy Apple Snow pudding Elle had deftly prepared. While in the kitchen to dole out the servings, she remembered the constable on duty. She prepared a basket and walked out the scullery and around the house to find him standing resolutely before their porch. He accepted the meal gratefully. When she returned to the kitchen she brought out the rest of the pudding to the dining table. The reception to the treat was gracious and appreciative.

"I feel we should invite the constable in for the night, but he refuses," Elle said as they enjoyed their pudding.

"Oh! The constable! I'd forgotten about his presence. Surely he can spend the evening with us?" Fidela said.

"Fidela!" Eden snorted. "Have such a common man keep us company?"

"He must stand at his station before our porch until the next policeman comes to replace him," Josefina said. "But he be making rounds outside, to keep us safe."

Pudding all eaten, Elle requested Austin's assistance in clearing the table so Josefina could continue her conversation about the gracious neighbours she'd met that day. Austin accommodated Elle's request with no fuss, and she thought that unlike English boys, he exhibited a helpful familiarity with handling dishes and moving about the kitchen that probably reflected a mother's diligence in giving her children chores. He even enquired about the washing up, and Elle said Mrs Willy's scullery girls would return to take care of that chore in the morning. What she didn't mention was that she'd made the inspectors promise that no-one in the Sundark would be present to prepare or enjoy luncheon.

When they returned to the dining room, Mr Hardwick placed his napkin on the table and rose.

"Would everyone like coffee?" Elle said. "Miss Dufish and I have a wonderful pot prepared, and the parlour would be an excellent spot to enjoy it in."

"With a card game, perhaps?" Austin said. "We could play Old Maid!"

"Eden is adept at cartomancy!" Fidela said. "Let's retire to the parlour then, where she can give her prognostications!"

"I'll be delighted to read the cards," Eden said. She rose regally. "After we've enjoyed our nightly viewing in the Dome." She swept by Fidela and departed the table.

Mr Hardwick said nothing and lurched after her. Josefina looked at Elle, shrugged, and followed her employer. Austin fell in step behind her. Elle was half of the mind to be rude and not join the others when Fidela touched her arm.

"Mrs Black, we're not occultists," she said. When Elle turned to look at Fidela, it seemed the older woman's gaze was pleading.

"Yes, Miss Sweetwater?" Elle said.

"I mean, we've never cast spells, never! Incantations and such workings! Nor cursed anyone! We're spiritualists!"

"Yet?" Elle prodded.

"*Fidela!*" Eden called from the reception area, her voice echoing. Austin looked back expectantly from the dining room door.

"She's been memorising the *voces magicae*, the words of power, in the book!" Fidela whispered harshly. She hastily departed for the door.

Elle looked at her in confusion. She exited the dining room to follow the group. Eden led the way, a silvery, wafting figure in her silk and turban. Fidela however, lagged in the rear, but when she looked at Elle, she refrained from speaking further.

As on the nights previous, the blue doors on the third floor swung silently open to admit them into the dome's darkness. Elle held her chatelaine still and moved quietly about the great space until she stood where Eden was plainly in her view. For even in the dark, Eden's silver hair and white-clad figure shone. Phosphorescence came to Elle's mind, recalling Austin's mention of that common medium's gimmick, but she strongly doubted Eden was doused in the substance.

Above and below them, the figures and designs glowed. The room rumbled. The dome cracked open.

The light of the stars and moon softly lit the upturned faces. Music played and the floor began its rotation. But while Elle steadied her feet she could see Fidela did not watch the sky; her fearful gaze was on Eden.

Eden stretched her arms out, her long sleeves spread wide, and spun around once, twice, then thrice.

"Hail! Hail! Hail! O night, night, night! Mighty Hekate of the Threshold!" she cried. "Beloved Goddess of the Crossroads and of the Three Ways! Night-going One, Protectress of dogs, Key-holding Mistress of our whole world! Reveal to me the divine pathways that I long for!"

"Eden, no!" Fidela said.

"Mr Washington, Mr Hardwick, we must remove Eden!" Elle sharply said. She leapt to lay hands on her but Eden evaded, running like a recalcitrant child around the group. She ran in a circle three times, emitting wild cries at each turn, even as Elle lunged by cutting across the bewildered bunch.

"What is happening?" Austin said.

"Are you silly birds conducting a summoning?" Mr Hardwick

said.

"I call upon you by all your holy names, Triple Hekate! In these you delight and in which we rejoice," Eden called loudly. "O Earthly One, Torch-Bearer, Unconquerable Queen! Ruler, Beast-Roarer, She who is before the Gate, our Saviour!"

"Mr Hardwick!" Elle shouted.

Mr Hardwick grabbed for Eden; his swiping arms caught air. To everyone's astonishment, Eden rose, feet dangling above ground. She floated for the open dome.

She spread her arms and feet and levitated higher. Austin jumped for her and landed on the floor, failing to grab hold. Elle quickly unfastened her chatelaine.

"Chthonia! Dadouchos! Enodia! Kleidouchos!" Eden cried, palms turned to the night sky.

"Propylaia! Soteira! Triformis! Troiditis!"

"Eden!" Fidela screamed.

Eden floated above, the locks of her hair and the fabric of her silks wafting like a bird's feathers in wind and in full wing. Her eyes shone and she pointed at Elle.

"Ablanathanalba," she intoned.

"Do not 'ablanathanalba' to me!" Elle said. She swung the weighted fob of her chatelaine and threw.

The chain wound around Eden's waist. Elle concentrated with all her might on the dangling crystal fob and mentally pulled. Eden jerked like a kite held up by too hard a wind to be forced down. Mr Hardwick grabbed the swinging tool ends. Arms outstretched, he lost his footing as Eden levitated higher. His shoes skidded on the rotating floor. Austin grabbed Mr Hardwick around the waist. With a cry, Josefina leapt on Austin's back. Their combined weights had no effect. Eden turned upright, arms and legs outstretched like the points of a star.

"He – – – – Askion!" Eden cried. "Kataskion, Lix Tetrax, *Dannameneus* A – -- — !"

The air loudly popped and Elle smelled deep earth. The hairs of her skin stood on end. Balls of blue fire erupted around Eden and descended on her body.

The fire enveloped her. Eden laughed, the sound nearly muted. Her shape distorted, and Elle felt she was viewing Eden through the smoke-filled doorway of an adjoining room, or as a reflection in a warped mirror.

"She accepts me!" Eden cried, her voice flat and faraway. "I am her—"

Elle saw Eden's expression change as her body shook mightily. Eden's face became a vibration of three faces, then six. Then, like night veils that swiftly drew shut, she and the fires winked out.

Something splattered wetly in the sudden dark. Mr Hardwick fell to the floor with Austin and Josefina atop, Elle's chatelaine collapsing in a jangling heap before him.

Elle smelled the metallic scent of fresh, slaughtered blood.

"Eden?" Fidela's quavering voice called.

Elle ran down the dark slope behind Sundark, nearly slipping in the dewy grass, her police lantern's light bobbing. Austin followed, protecting the flame of a candle with a cupped hand. They stopped at the chained gate of the walled garden, and Elle gave the padlock a focused stare. It clicked apart and dangled. She pulled the chain off and they hurried inside.

The smell of moist earth and electrical storms filled the air. Moonlight shown softly on the soil and still plants, turning all a night-grey. Elle and Austin showed their lights on the rows. They stumbled on holes and uneven soil. Elle saw moonlight reflect on a scalp of wavy, fine silver, sat like a hare hiding amongst the turnips.

"Here she is," Elle said soberly.

Eden's head was fully buried, only her shining hair above ground. Elle had a sudden, morbid impulse to touch the scalp, just to feel if the skin were still warm. She heard Austin stumble back, trip over Eden's turban amongst the carrots, and retch.

When Elle and Austin returned to the garden entrance, Mr Hardwick leaned on the gate. His deep breaths misted in the air, and he wiped his sleeve on his sweating forehead. Eden's blood stiffened his hair.

He stared at them. Elle passed without a word, leaving Austin to deal with his questions. She saw the constable with his own lit lantern hurry down the slope. Josefina stood on the terrace leading to the ballroom's French doors, peering down at Elle and her light.

She looked at Elle's face, nodded stiffly, and hurried back inside.

The constable stopped before Elle. She looked up at him.

"She didn't quite make it to Venus," she said.

CHAPTER EIGHT

My Darling Fae',
I've had enough of this business. I've lost Miss Eden Brunch despite my efforts. And this, after having Mr and Mrs Willy, who were of hotel staff, removed by the police, as it appeared they might have been responsible for other guests vanishing. But I never suspected so. The two picked up the guests' pieces when they ended up in the garden—and looted them and their remaining belongings! But I concurred with their protestations. Whatever did all this is—well, it's that which took Miss Brunch.

This time I saw the manner of the vanishing. This is not about a faulty portal to Venus, or preternatural workings towards alchemical transcendence. This is the work of life-eating malevolence. The aforementioned goddess in my last letter runs rampant here, to deleterious effect.

I had made a private agreement with our inspectors to have us, every single one, leave this place in the morning. But this recent event meant summoning the police—whomever could drag themselves from their warm beds—to return tonight. We are packing now. The denizens of Sundark make even this simple task difficult.

Miss Sweetwater has rendered herself insensate from soothing syrup, no doubt from the loss of Miss Brunch. Mr Washington is vigorously evading efforts to accost him, and Mr Hardwick is nowhere to be seen, but I've at least forced Miss Dufish to pack, because when she leaves, Mr Washington will leave—despite the fact that he witnessed the comforting hand clasp Josefina gave the despondent Mr Hardwick when the police dug up parts of Miss Brunch. Mr Washington is understandably upset by that unfortunate demonstration, but I don't believe he'll remain stubborn—unlike a certain hotel owner. I've plans for dealing with that bull-headed Mr Hardwick.

The police will transport us to the hotel in Bromley Town where we'll remain under house arrest. For we are now all suspects in Mr Lunt and Miss Brunch's murders, is that not amusing?

My Heart, you will receive this letter swiftly thanks to the police messenger dispatched tonight to Met headquarters in Whitehall Place. He has graciously agreed to do me the favour of riding his wheel to our house and delivering this personally to you.

Beloved, I will join you soon. Know that I love you more and more. How lucky I am, and would attest to God my gratitude every day—every minute, every waking moment!—that you were willing to love and marry so morbid and mad a widow!

In Gratitude to my Love,
Your Eleanor

Elle had drunk one can of feverfew tea, two cans of Faedra's coffee, and one cup of the brew she and Josefina had made before the ill-fated conclusion of dinner. She'd packed her cases, wiped Eden's blood off her broken chatelaine, and had stowed that, the remaining can of tea, and her knitting in her carpetbag. Many of the links of her "detecting equipage" had broken or been weakened by the combined weight of three earnest people. But she knew Faedra would find the damage an exciting prospect for rebuilding. She ate the last of the chocolates, pocketed her last can of coffee, donned her cape and bonnet, and carried her cases down.

She met two constables on their way up to gather the remaining guests, and they helpfully took her luggage for her. She then went down to the kitchen to drink another cup of coffee and enjoy leftover Hoppin' John.

Dawn found her standing on the back terrace as the morning's light slowly crept over the silent land and trees. Birds began their activity. She read from Fidela's book, noting the words from hymns and spells that Eden had pieced together to form her own invocation. But a chapter caught her eye regarding the strophalos, or 'magic wheel' of Hekate that Fidela had named. Elle read:

" . . . *as Eusebius noted in his* Praeparatio Evangelica, *the old gods were susceptible to compulsion, guised as persuasive prayer, and thus could be forcibly summoned down, as with such devises of magic like the wheels of mystical charm."*

"Forcibly compelled?" Elle said. She heard the creak of the barn door below and looked up.

She watched the police, two inspectors and two constables, leave the barn where Eden Brunch's freshly retrieved body parts awaited the doctor. They walked up the slope for Sundark.

The men grimly touched their hats as they neared. Elle pocketed the HEKATE book, nodded to them, turned, and preceded them into the house.

But as she passed through the French doors she heard large dogs bark, deep and powerfully, the sound echoing somewhere beyond the barn. She frowned, wondering why she'd never heard dogs before. She led the police through the ballroom for the reception area.

Josefina stood outside her office by her packed bags. Austin lingered near, hands in his pockets. His hat was stained dark by the blood that had splattered when Eden's "transport to Venus" ended. Elle wondered if he realised it was soiled. Considering his obstinate refusal to ever take the hat off, she wouldn't be surprised if he knew perfectly well that it was in ghastly condition.

Josefina, tight-lipped and disapproving, merely watched as Elle, with the police following, approached the calling tube by the ascension chamber's gate. Elle pulled down the lever to activate it.

"Mr Hardwick," she said into the tube. "I must speak to you about your wife."

The cables of the ascension chamber started, and Elle watched the counterweight swiftly drop. When the room arrived, she drew back the gate for the policemen and shut it after them.

As the men descended, Elle turned to Josefina and Austin.

"Now, won't you two board our carriage outside?" she said.

"Well," Austin said, looking at Josefina.

"A full breakfast awaits us at the hotel in Bromley Town," Elle coaxed.

"Mr Hardwick should not be removed in such a manner, Mrs Black," Josefina said sternly. "Like some criminal! Until I see that the police be treating him with respect, I will not abandon him."

"It's not abandonment, Miss Dufish, it's merely a brief separation where you step away, as you would when your employer is in the water closet. In this case, he is being fetched from his closet while you wait *outside*."

Josefina raised her chin and continued to keep her attention on the ascension area's gate. Elle rolled her eyes.

"If you two do not depart, this instant," she said, raising her voice, "I will have no choice but to call upon my powers and—"

Josefina picked up her skirts and hurried from the reception area and down the hall. Austin grabbed Josefina's bags and ran after her.

Elle took a breath. She entered the office, where she knew there was a water closet.

After Elle emerged from the lavatory, feeling refreshed and rather fancying another cup of coffee, she saw Josefina and Austin standing in the reception area again.

"Did I just dream?" Elle said.

"I forgot me parasol," Josefina said, exhibiting the object in question.

"Mr Washington," Elle said patiently. "I know your equipment is now outside, why don't we add Miss Dufish's luggage so that the drivers may load them?"

"I'll do so gladly," Austin said. He picked up the suitcases again.

"Mr Hardwick has still not ascended," Josefina said tersely.

"No doubt he is showing the inspectors the inner workings of Sundark," Elle said.

"I wouldn't be surprised. For as long as I've stayed here, that's all he seems to do! Work on those tarnal engines." Austin turned to Josefina. "Miss Dufish . . . he's just that sort of widower. A one-woman man. He won't change."

Josefina looked at him indignantly.

"He be my employer, Mr Washington, and me not appreciating your insinuation!" she snapped.

"Insinuation? I think your answer rather affirms everything!" Austin huffed.

"Mr Washington," Elle loudly interrupted. "I'll accompany you out, for I need to see if Miss Sweetwater is comfortable in the carriage."

Austin turned and marched for the hotel entrance, his footsteps echoing.

But once outside, Austin promptly dropped the bags on the drive and hurried up the porch steps before Elle could stop him. She would have pursued except she noticed that one of the constables meant to fetch Fidela was standing on the drive, their luggage still in a pile, and not one carriage could be seen.

"What happened to our transport?" Elle said. "Has Miss Sweetwater been taken away already?"

"Ma'am, the horses were too nervous to remain," the constable said. He was the large fellow who guarded them last night, and his baggy eyes and weary face attested to his long vigil without sleep. "All our wagons are down below, on the road. The horses would not stay after hearing the strange hounds."

"Hounds," Elle said. "I didn't think they barked like hounds."

"You're right, ma'am. I've seen 'em, big black dogs, ma'am,"

Mr Arch's boy piped up. Elle had not noticed him crouching near the round porch with the witch's dome. He was freckled-faced and appeared more refreshed, Elle thought, than any of the adults present right then. He stuffed a penny dreadful into his back pocket and stood. "They're running in the woods behind the stables and they're big as bears. They just appeared, ma'am! And they were black! The neighbours never said they'd be having such animals."

"Black dogs are favoured by Hekate," Elle said. "I'm certain they'll have three heads each, next. Then Mr Arch must be at the foot of the hill with the Sundark's horses, is that correct?" The boy nodded. "No need to run down to summon them back for us, we'll walk down. With such strange dogs about, I want you to go right now and rejoin the drivers."

The boy smiled in relief, touched his cap, and ran down the hill for the tree-lined drive and its black entrance gate.

"But Miss Sweetwater is with the drivers, isn't she?" Elle said, turning to the constable. He looked at her sheepishly.

"I've a man at her door, ma'am. She's still in her room." He leaned down to whisper self-consciously. "She's still in her sleeping things."

"I see," Elle said with a tired smile. "Then I'll return upstairs with you and make certain she's made respectable for travel."

She mounted the stairs ahead of the constable. As she reached for the doorknob, the doors suddenly flew inward.

Elle felt a chilled wind rush in from behind her, pulled into the hall like a frost giant's sucking inhalation. Her skirts flapped. They dropped when the wind left as suddenly as it had come.

"Like a stampede o'er me grave," the constable softly exclaimed.

"Spectral wind," Elle mused. "But why—"

She felt a silent scream build from within the house, just as it had done when she had first approached the Sundark by carriage. A deep, expanding wail grew and swelled. It burst down the hall and hurtled towards them, a white rush of wide-mouthed spectres.

Elle spun around and smacked into the constable's chest. His arms instinctively went around her.

She felt a blow into her back like a runaway train.

When she came to her senses, she was in the drive, lying atop the still bulk of the constable. Her bonnet had rolled down the hill. The policeman's helmet lay a yard away, and she saw the blood staining the paving stone beneath his head. Strangely, more blood was on his silver badge, though she thought his pale face was undamaged.

Something hot ran down the side of her face and trickled into her collar. She touched her forehead, and her fingers came away red with blood.

She stumbled to her feet and turned around. The Sundark spun like a mad carousel.

Fists clenched, she tried to discern the location of the portico entrance. Windows, doors, steps, pillars—they flew by her sight like objects swept up in a cyclone.

"You can't sustain such antics forever!" Elle said. She reeled slightly. "And when you take a breath, for at some point you must—I'll be ready for you!"

She threw off her cape. She ran as fast as she could around the side of the house.

Only a few yards from the Sundark's great black gates, a hackney carriage came to a stop. Faedra looked out the window and saw a police wagon, two carriages—one bearing the mark of Sundark—a stable boy minding a horse, and another small wagon where two kitchen maids sat. Everyone was pointing up the hill and discussing things animatedly.

"What's happened?" Faedra called up to her driver. She tamped down her sudden dread. He leaned over and pointed.

"Well, it appears the gates are locked, ma'am. See there, those police drivers are trying to get them open," he said. Just as he indicated, Faedra saw the men who were shaking the black bars of the great gate, to no avail.

"The gates aren't locked!" the stable boy said. He approached them, bringing along his docile horse. "They just won't open! They slammed shut just as I'd come through. I was lucky not to be trapped on the other side with those big black dogs roaming about."

"Black dogs?" Faedra said.

"Yes, ma'am! Big ones, the size of horses! They came from nowhere!"

"You're a very observant lad," Faedra said, resisting the urge to fly out of the carriage and shake the bars as well. She mustered a smile for the boy. He beamed up at her. "Can you tell me if Mrs Black has already departed the Sundark? She's meant to be in Bromley Town. She's a woman younger than myself, with dark-red hair and eyes made dark with kohl."

"Oh, her! She's not come down yet, ma'am. Nor the others staying at the Sundark. And now the house is spinning again!"

"Spinning?" Faedra said. The boy pointed up the hill.

Faedra looked up through the trees but could not discern what the others saw. She encouraged the boy to tell her something of what the property was like over the wall and gave him a coin for his trouble. Thus, she instructed her driver to take her farther down the road, past the police wagons, and to follow Sundark's stone wall. Once out of sight from the drivers, she quickly climbed up her carriage and leapt from it for the wall.

She dropped herself over the side while her driver continued to Bromley Town. Faedra sped through the woods for where the Sundark house would be. When the house came into sight, she finally saw what the boy had been speaking of.

A tornado seemed to possess the house, only one that was made of ghost house parts that flew around like the fleeting pictures on a spinning top's sides. Faedra shivered.

"Elle," she said, and started up the hill. She heard dogs bay in the far distance and moved faster.

On the other side of Sundark, Elle peered out of the barn's doors.

She saw the Sundark stop spinning and flung the doors open.

Elle trundled Mr Willy's barrow up the slope. Her neck was draped with four of Heric's escapist chains. More lay inside the barrow. Her activated coffee can was piping-hot inside her dress pocket. She had drunk half of the coffee while in the barn, and then heard the deep barking of large dogs, but those did not concern her right then.

"We're a train!" she chanted under her breath. "A train! A train!"

She imagined the barrow as a locomotive. When she reached the back veranda, she ran forwards as fast as she could. The barrow left her grasp and hurtled towards the French doors with the full force of her mental power.

The resulting crash splintered wood and sent glass flying. Elle kept the barrow moving with her mind. She passed through the broken doors just as they tried to swing shut. She ran down the ballroom with the barrow rolling madly before her.

She allowed the barrow to crash into the office in the reception area and remain there. The ascension chamber had not returned, and Josefina and Austin were nowhere to be seen.

Elle took a breath and pulled a length of chain from her neck. She ran down the hall and through the drawing room for the main staircase. A sudden boom sounded. The resulting tremor shook the house and nearly made Elle lose her feet.

It had felt as if a cannon had been shot somewhere below her. She leapt for the steps. The air grew colder as she climbed. She heard a high-pitched screeching, winding in and out of her aural perception.

"Oh, you are in a mood," Elle said. She pressed her back to the wall, the chain held in both her hands, and ascended to the second floor.

The hallway pulsated. The gaslights died and then burst to life erratically. Elle saw shadows flicker and run along the breathing walls. She stepped into the hall and more shadows flitted beneath her feet. She ignored them and their screechy sounds, like fingernails on a chalkboard.

She ran for Fidela's room at the far end next to the gold door. Just as she reached her goal, her world blinked and—

The gold door, once shut, was then ajar. She saw a man's trembling legs and feet as he was dragged through the opening. He screamed. It was the constable left with Fidela.

The gold door slammed shut. Elle pulled it open. She saw nothing but darkness. With the chain in a raised fist, she advanced, then abruptly halted.

"No," she said.

She turned instead to Fidela's door, raised her skirts, and kicked hard.

When the door swung open, she felt that she'd burst an aural bubble. Elle was assaulted by the sound of Fidela screaming. Balls of blue flame surrounded the spinster as she huddled in her nightclothes on the bed. Elle flung her chain.

She sent it arcing through the blue fires, end over end, scattering them. With a mental command she forced the chain to swerve around Fidela and whip back, dispelling the remaining flames. The chain hurtled towards Elle and she stepped aside. It smashed against the doorframe. The atmosphere in the room suddenly lightened and the fires winked out.

Elle hurried to the bed and abruptly slipped. When she looked down, she saw a puddle of fresh blood on the floor.

"The constable was taken!" Fidela cried, her pale face stricken. Her nightclothes were rumpled and her loose grey hair was in disarray.

"I thought as much," Elle said grimly. "And now, Miss Sweetwater, I must take you!" She grabbed Fidela and pulled her out of the bed. She flung a blanket over Fidela's shoulders. "I apologise for not garbing you sensibly, but we must leave."

"Oh, Mrs Black, your head is injured! Are you dead?"

A loud boom shook the house. The room rattled and Fidela

looked about dazedly.

Too much syrup! Elle thought. She took a breath.

"If I were, Miss Sweetwater, I would be hovering over my wife and not here, addressing the strange issues of this house." She directed them towards the door.

"I slept!" Fidela said as Elle led them out. "Because by awakening . . . Eden might be here again."

"I understand," Elle said. "I had once done the same."

"I still don't want to wake," Fidela said. She put her head in her hands and her feet slowed.

"Then consider this a continuance of your dream. Look!" Elle pulled the HEKATE book from her skirt's pocket. "I have brought you your book! Now come, our carriage awaits and we can discuss everything there." She thrust the book into Fidela's hands and marched her quickly down the hall.

"Eden always had abilities, how we rejoiced when we found that the Sundark made her long-time gifts apparent!" Fidela said. As they hurried, Elle looked about. The hall, silent except for their rapid steps, appeared innocuous. She saw no breathing walls or flitting shadows.

"I watched her grow powerful with each day!" Fidela said. "But now I understand! She was allowed to become thus so that the Sundark could feast on her!"

Elle dragged Fidela down the stairs.

"I helped to kill Eden!"

"I disagree, but you may remonstrate with me all you want once we're outside," Elle said as she pulled her along.

"Mrs Black, the black sun won't just facilitate the dissolution of our bodies! It will eat us all!"

"Not myself, Fidela! I drink far too much feverfew tea and am therefore quite bitter-tasting."

She hurried Fidela across the drawing room and brought them to a halt in the hallway. She assessed the front entrance and her choices. Fetching her barrow, she thought, might be the wiser move.

Another boom from below sounded. The floor and walls shook

and she helped Fidela keep her feet.

"Heavens," Elle murmured, wondering if this was what the fabled California earthquakes felt like.

"Eden!" Fidela cried.

Elle turned. A white-robed figure with a turban passed quickly through the reception area.

Fidela broke from Elle's grasp and ran for where the figure had been.

"No, Fidela! That's—"

Elle pursued, but Fidela's passion made her faster. Fidela reached the centre of the reception area and suddenly flew straight up as if grabbed by a giant invisible hand. Her bare feet kicked.

"No!" Elle cried. She reached with her hands and mind. The HEKATE book burst in a flurry of torn pages. Fidela disappeared from her sight as if a curtain of air had drawn shut around her.

Blood fell down. It landed in the very centre of the reception area and splattered Elle's dress. She trembled, her hands still grasping for Fidela amidst the fluttering paper.

"I will see to your *destruction!*" Elle shouted, stamping her foot.

The sound of her heel echoed in the reception area. As she seethed, she heard a loud crack.

She looked about. She heard another, glanced up, and saw the dome's glass crawling with cracks.

Elle ran to the office doorway and her barrow. Braced against the doorframe, she felt another loud boom shake the floor beneath her feet. She heard both the dome and reception area floor crack apart and collapse in a loud thunder of raining glass and crumbling concrete. Clouds of dust rose.

Elle coughed and covered her face until the air cleared. She heard machinery work and the alarmed sounds of people shouting at each other.

When she looked up again, the reception area was piled with rubble and glass, but in the very centre was a gaping hole. She picked her way cautiously to the edge and peered down.

From the reception floor slab down to the cavern Mr Hardwick laboured in, Elle saw solid machinery. Burst electric cables sparked and steam roiled from punctured pipes. Thirty feet below, she saw the great engine room's floor, the machines no longer orderly. They had grown, erupting like invasive plants from the floor and walls. Cables writhed. She saw Mr Hardwick, gesturing helplessly, a small stick of dynamite in his hand. In his other fist he clenched several more. He was watching Josefina and Austin, who were clinging to each other as a tall, mechanical heap of turning gears and churning pistons moved towards them.

Elle grabbed a length of chain from her neck and hurled it down.

With a mental command, she curved the chain's flight until it struck the advancing machine in its cogs, tangling them. A loud, painful screech sounded as the machinery jammed. It halted and shuddered and Josefina and Austin hurried away. Elle went back to her barrow and pushed it through the rubble to the edge of the pit. She pulled out chains and threw them, mentally aiming her projectiles for any moving parts. As she wedged engines at random, one exploded, spewing bolts and the rubber bits of turning belts. Mr Hardwick looked up, incredulous.

"Feel my thunderbolts!" she said. She flung her last chain from the barrow and mentally directed it at the last lumbering machine.

"Miss Dufish, Mr Washington! Return upstairs at once!" she called as the machine chewed on her chain, belched, and became inert.

"Mrs Black, we can't!" Josefina yelled amid the smoke that arose. "Machinery come through the walls of the stairs we descended from! There be no more stairs!"

"And the ascension room?" Elle said.

"The roof's collapse has buried it!" Austin shouted.

"And the policemen?" Elle called.

Only the sound of struggling machinery answered her. With a howl, Mr Hardwick turned, lit the wick of his stick of dynamite and threw it out of Elle's line of sight. He spread his arms in the direction of the forthcoming blast, like one welcoming his imminent demise.

Elle gritted her teeth and grabbed hold of Mr Hardwick with her mind. She mentally dragged his bulk back by only a few feet then made him fall on his behind as the house shook from another booming explosion. Mr Hardwick looked around him and then up at her. Gears and other broken hardware flew and landed on the ground. A cloud of dust rose.

Elle laughed suddenly, and the sound echoed against the reception area walls. Her burst of mirth sounded uncannily like those she had emitted when she was in the asylum.

"I daresay I've had one cup too many," she said.

She heard Josefina shriek. When she looked their way, blue fires held Austin aloft.

She removed a chain from her neck and flung it down at Austin.

At such a distance and under dim light, she hoped to not accidentally strike and kill him. She set her jaw and flew the chain around his struggling form until all the blue fires burst on contact and dispelled. She allowed the chain to fling itself away. Austin fell in a heap, holding on to the hat firmly set on his head.

"Thank you!" he shouted up to Elle.

If I leave for a ladder or a rope, the house will surely end them, she thought.

She held the remaining chain around her neck.

"Mr Hardwick! I am about to fall like Sir Isaac Newton's apple!" she called down. He took to his feet and shouted in alarm. Elle stepped out and promptly fell.

CHAPTER NINE

When Faedra saw Elle's bonnet lazily rolling this way, then
that way, down the hill to the whims of the breeze, she gave a
strangled cry and chased it. Then she crushed the bonnet against
her breast. Fear gave her sufficient impetus to barrel up the hill.
The hotel had ceased spinning when she'd been at the hill's foot,
and Faedra saw then that the house had been under a supernatural
illusion. It appeared, to her relief, to have no damage whatsoever
to its exterior. Her relief was short-lived when she heard a dull
boom. It sounded similar to cannon fire and made her hurry
more. Halfway up the hill, she heard a second explosion, and
then a third and a fourth once she surmounted the top. When she
saw the prone constable, the evidence of his head wound staining
the stones, and Elle's cape flung to the ground, she halted in her
rally to reach the front porch.

"You must have judged it imperative to re-enter the house,"
Faedra said breathlessly as she detoured to see to the unconscious
constable. She fell to her knees beside him. "Or else you wouldn't

have left this poor fellow like this. I hope he's not dead."

She lifted one of his eyelids, tested his faint breath's issue on her wrist, and then examined his head. She had packed a small medical kit in Elle's luggage and went to retrieve it.

After quickly bandaging the unconscious constable and pillowing his head with Elle's folded cape, she heard yet another boom. It rattled the windows. Faedra abandoned her nursing and leapt for the porch. She tried the handles of the front doors. They did not appear locked, for she could turn them easily, but the doors refused to open despite how hard she pushed. She peered into the plate glass and saw nothing in the dim hallway.

"The windows," she said.

She hurried for the bay window beneath the witch's hat dome. Two windows that were long and narrow were unlatched and ajar. She reached for them.

They suddenly slammed shut as if pulled by an invisible hand. Faedra snatched her fingers back.

After a moment of staring at the glass in surprise, she went to the porch's rocking chair. She drew breath and lifted it. Just as she was about to swing it at the bay window, regretting that she had to destroy such beautiful art glass, she heard the pounding approach of great dogs.

Large black dogs burst around the corner of the house and barked. Faedra dropped the chair and scurried back. She reached into her bustle and pulled out her silver Smith & Wesson.

Before she could take aim another black dog rounded the corner. Faedra froze, for not only was it the biggest but it bore three heads, their three jaws gnashing.

Elle knew that by falling thirty feet, the force of her body would be too much for even Mr Hardwick to bear. Machinery blurred past her sight as she imagined a cushion of helium gas around her, lifting her mass. She slowed her descent only by a margin.

I'm a feather! Feather! Feather! She thought, concentrating hard. Balls of blue fire flickered to life around her falling form. She heard Josefina scream in alarm.

Try your hand, she thought at the blue fires.

But the blue flames winked out and Elle fell freely. She felt herself land in Mr Hardwick's arms and his great "oof" of exhalation. The force of her descent sent him nearly to the floor as he caught her to him.

"Now you've done it! You're trapped down here with us!" he exclaimed as she disengaged.

"We'll not be trapped for long, Mr Hardwick, for we are all leaving, right this minute!" Elle said.

"Not I. Someone must stop all of this. Whatever your fantastic escape plan is, take the others and go! Before that grievous head wound addles your good senses further!" Mr Hardwick turned and pulled out dynamite sticks from a trouser pocket. He proceeded to light one with a match.

"Give me those!" Elle snatched them out of his hands. Tucking them into the back of her skirt's waistband, she brandished the lit one at Mr Hardwick. "My good senses! Who is attempting to collapse the very house on himself?"

"Mrs Black!" Austin yelled in alarm. "That's dynamite!"

She wet her fingers with her tongue and pinched the fuse's flame. It extinguished in a puff of smoke.

"I know, Mr Washington, they're the same sort used at excavation sites, though thankfully these tiny things look fresh and have yet to weep nitroglycerin," she said as she brought the stick up for closer scrutiny.

"Tiny—they were all I had!" Mr Hardwick sputtered. "I *am* trying to stop the house, Mrs Black!"

"Did this only occur to you now, great engineer that you are?" Elle said as she stuck the extinguished stick in her waistband with the others.

"It occurred to me weeks ago, you silly bird!" he bellowed. "I have been gutting the machinery every night! None of this should be moving at all!"

Elle took hold of Mr Hardwick's hand and pulled him to follow her. She marched directly for the trapped ascension chamber.

"Mr Washington, Miss Dufish!" she called. "Help clear the chamber's roof of debris, if you please!"

"Oh, and shall we ascend for tea, then?" Mr Hardwick said as their companions scrambled to do as bidden. "Perhaps to discuss my wife? That was a very good trick, Mrs Black. When I saw the men I welcomed being arrested! But the damn house would not have it! So here I am, a true killer, unable to save them! Not to mention all the wretched rest, my own guests!"

Elle set her jaw and pulled Mr Hardwick along.

"You may ask yourself, 'Why does he still resist departure?'" he continued. "Would it not follow that I would weary of my gruesome role of Reaper? Shouldn't I desire sweet freedom from this guilt, this millstone of personal terror? But even if you had me dragged away in chains, it will not end, Mrs Black! It will never end!"

"Mr Hardwick, I will gladly listen to your redresses at another time! But right now, pick up those lagging big feet!"

He pulled his hand out of her grasp.

"Are you truly a witch?" he demanded. "Have you any sorcery beyond juggling dishes? Because that's what's needed, Mrs Black. Damned witchcraft! I've tried breaking the machines, now use those esemplastic powers! Break the sorcery that rules this house!"

"Very well!" Elle said. "Come with me!"

"Did you not hear —"

"I did, and I said, 'Come with me', Mr Hardwick!" Elle snapped. "If you had not been focused solely on the engines and your silly guilt, you might have deduced this for yourself!"

She pulled off her last length of chain, still silvery and bright despite the grime on it. When she'd seen it she knew it was Heric's best, performing restraint.

She threw it at Mr Hardwick and with a concentrated thought, wrapped it around his torso and pinned his arms. The padlock clicked shut against his chest.

"*Everyone* must leave this house, Mr Hardwick!" Elle said. "Every single person! For a house has no reason to exist unless someone is living in it!"

The ground shuddered beneath them. The tremors escalated until Elle was forced to hold on to Mr Hardwick.

"Did you set more explosives?" she demanded.

"I did not!" Mr Hardwick said.

Elle grabbed him by the chain and they ran together, over debris and struggling, broken machinery. Josefina and Austin hurriedly descended from the ascension chamber's roof to avoid falling off. Elle felt their shaking floor collapse. She looked behind her and saw concrete crumble and dust clouds rise where she and Mr Hardwick had stood. A gaping hole, directly below the one above, had formed.

"There are more floors?" Elle coughed, waving the dust of debris away from her.

"No! I've—I had no idea there was even more below this!" Mr Hardwick said in surprise.

Elle felt Josefina and Austin hurry to her side. She and the others leaned over the new pit and peered through the remaining dust.

"What can be down there?" Austin asked.

"It be sounding like more machines!" Josefina said.

Mr Hardwick gasped.

Elle stared into the dimness. Far below, she distinguished the outline of an emaciated female form. She was a dry, hollow-eyed husk dressed in a ragged, black lace, crinoline dress, her slack-jawed face still framed by strands of oily black curls. She lay cradled in a metal, mechanical coffin tangled in electrical wires and cables that pierced what was left of her flesh. Minute lights flickered from gaps in her dress and within her eye sockets.

"There you are!" Elle shouted. "You show yourself at last? Goddess trapper! Murderess!"

"Alana!" Mr Hardwick cried.

Elle looked at him in surprise.

"Mrs Black, you were right! My wife is as dead as your own husband, planted beneath the ground. And what is the duty of a surviving husband but that he should see to his wife, even into the beyond!" Mr Hardwick shouted into the pit. "Take me, then! Let the murders *end!*"

"That is not your wife, Mr Hardwick!" Elle said.

Hardwick swivelled to look at her.

"That corpse is not your wife, unless she preferred wearing dresses that were the fashion forty years ago!"

He gaped at her.

"And hasn't your wife *red hair?*" Elle said incredulously.

"That—be *Mrs Sundark!*" Josephina cried.

As if in response, the machines churned. Gears grinded and screamed, and Elle thought the lights within Abigail's skull grew brighter.

"Why did you believe that your wife was causing the disappearances, Mr Hardwick?" Elle said. "Did you pursue Heric and Abigail Sundark's secrets for that purpose? Did you help Alana become part of the house?"

"No!" he said in astonishment. "Never! I only loved the machines, and she the Dome!"

"Then think no more that your wife is here, for she is not, nor is she behind the evil of this house!" Elle said. "If you are guilty of anything, it was acting as that corpse's Hephaestus and encouraging its passion for you!"

Mr Hardwick's jaw dropped.

"Did your man leave you?" Elle cried down into the pit. "Is that what he did, when you became too much for him? *When he realised you were a murderess?*"

"Mr Hardwick is *not* your man!" Josefina said.

The ground shook suddenly. The machines surrounding Abigail's corpse stirred and with jerking motions, seemed to grow. Wires and cables appeared and slowly snaked.

"Destroy her with dynamite, Mrs Black!" Josefina demanded, pointing at the corpse.

"I would, but if the house destroys itself along with her, we should not be here when that happens," Elle said.

The others looked at her in dismay.

"Is that not electrical?" Elle then said, pointing at the fine wires and cables leading to Abigail Sundark's skull.

"Those are much like . . . a helm of mental command!" Mr Hardwick said. "But the electrical pulses of control are somehow directly married with her once-flesh, a symbiotic—"

Elle pulled out her coffee can, sloshing with liquid. She grabbed hold of Mr Hardwick, leaned out as far as she could, and poured coffee down the pit. The long, thin stream dribbled on the corpse's head.

Wires popped and smoke rose. The corpse's bony limbs jiggled noisily as if it were being electrocuted.

The lights and gas flames in the pit dimmed just as the ones in the chamber dropped in intensity and nearly flickered out. The machines grew silent. The corpse stilled.

"You could have thrown a rock at her skull and perhaps achieved the same!" Mr Hardwick said, his voice echoing in the sudden quiet.

"Well, she's lucky I'd the coffee, I would have pissed on her instead!" Elle said.

"*Mrs Black!*" Josefina said in shock.

"To the ascension room!" Elle ordered. "While she is blinded or however I've addled her!"

"But the room is still—" Austin said. Elle prodded him.

"Everyone must take hold of Mr Hardwick and go!" she said.

They ran over the debris and inert machinery amid steam escaping. The ascension chamber was buried in fallen rubble, but the roof was cleared and the upper half was visible. Elle directed everyone to climb on top, dragging the chained Mr Hardwick up. When all were stood on top of the chamber, the ground began shaking again. Elle looked at Mr Hardwick.

"It's not my doing, you've my dynamite and I'm chained up!" he said. "And why is it everyone is holding on to me, the prisoner, as if I were a life raft?"

"Because, Mr Hardwick, she will not try to kill us as long as we are with you!" Elle said. She then held on tighter as the shaking grew.

More of the floor crumbled and machinery collapsed into

the widening pit. A piston suddenly churned. A deep clanking sounded as machinery came to life, spat out twisted and melted chain links, and whirred into motion once more. The group clung to each other and heard a woman's laughter, deep in the darkness below.

"Ha!" Elle said. "I've heard better laughter in the asylum. Often emitted by myself."

"If she starts speaking, you must throw dynamite at her, Mrs Black!" Josefina nervously said. The space shook more and the floor crumbled further. The abyss widened and grew closer to the trapped ascension chamber. Pistons suddenly appeared from within the pit, churning. The sound of machinery became a din. Steam shot into the air.

"Tarnation! How can it keep growing?" Austin exclaimed. He ducked as an electrical cable dropped and curled. Josefina smacked it away.

Elle turned and saw Mr Hardwick, his eyes bleak. She thought the look was familiar and inexplicably, she recalled a piano playing.

"I told you it would not end," he said.

He flexed his arms, the muscles of his neck taut and straining. The chains across his chest burst.

"Mr Hardwick!" Elle cried as he flung his restraints off. "Come back at once!"

"I will go to your Venus, Sundark witch!" he bellowed to the churning abyss. "And if a lyre need be played, I'll play it for you, Alana, and lead you back out of hell again! I will not leave you in there with that demoness, alone!"

Mr Hardwick looked at his companions.

"Josefina," he said. "My friend. Give Mrs Black her sum for the widows and orphans fund."

He turned and jumped. The clanking dark swallowed him.

"*Mr Hardwick!*" Josefina screamed.

Elle leaned out and stared down into the dark. Far below, she saw blue fires erupt and envelope Mr Hardwick's suspended form. He floated above the corpse of Abigail Sundark. Elle saw him like a warped mirror's reflection. His body became a vibration of three, then six.

Elle pulled out the dynamite stick from her waistband. She turned and lit the fuse with the sparks of grinding gears edging towards them. It flared upon igniting.

"Oh Lord, Mrs Black!" Austin cried. He gripped the rooftop and hugged Josefina tight against him.

"Mrs Black, no!" Josefina said. "Mr Hardwick—"

"Has gone to Venus, Miss Dufish," Elle said.

She bent over the side and tossed the stick into the gate of the ascension chamber. She turned and held on to the rooftop and her companions.

A boom deafened her ears and the resulting force buckled the metal beneath their feet. It blew the debris away from the rupturing ascension room. Elle saw the counterweight above rapidly descend just as they and their chamber shot up into the air and into the reception area's sunlight.

The counterweight crashed into the rubble of the reception area floor. The ascension room jiggled to a stop within the ascension area's gate, flinging Elle to the jagged floor and nearly back into the abyss below. The hole belched steam. She forced her aching body to rise and found her ankle caught.

When she looked back, she saw a black cable curled around her leg. She felt it pull. She clawed the floor for purchase as the cable dragged her back to the pit.

"Mrs Black!" Josefina cried. She and Austin hurried in their climb down the ascension area's iron housing.

Elle heard the howl of great dogs. She turned her head to the sound of thundering paws and scratching claws in the hallway. A giant black dog with three heads burst into the reception area.

It ran for Elle. One of the huge heads reached down and bit the cable in two.

Elle took to her feet only to fall flat again as more snaking cables shot over her head. The dog's heads snarled and ferociously barked. It bit at the reaching cables and Elle scrambled away. With a great leap, the dog dove into the pit.

"Mrs Black!" Josefina said. She and Austin ran up. The reception area echoed with fierce barking.

"I am well! Mr Washington, Miss Dufish, take yourselves out of this house, now!" Elle shouted. "You cannot be present for what I'm about to do!"

The two stared at her. Elle waved her arms and, laughed maniacally, rivalling Abigail's own echoing laughter that suddenly sounded in the reception area.

Josefina and Austin turned and ran down the hallway.

Faedra's intention to shoot died when she saw the barking dogs break formation and circle her while the three-headed dog came to a halt and stared. Flustered by the intelligence she could see in the dog's three pairs of staring eyes, Faedra kept her pistol up. Then it stood on its hind legs and knocked her down.

Faedra landed heavily, still holding her pistol away, and when she finally shoved her hat from her eyes she saw the three-headed dog standing above, its four great paws planted. Its three heads looked off into the distance as if listening to invisible masters.

"Play 'statue' elsewhere! Let me up!" she commanded, but she knew she'd lost all authority once she'd allowed the beast to push her.

After a few futile attempts to budge the oblivious creature, Faedra went to her belly and crawled out, only for one of the dogs to come, tail wagging, and flop across her back and lie down. She marshalled strength, heaved its heavy body aside, but before she could rise, the rest tackled her. They wrestled with her as if she were a littermate. Despite being knocked about, she held her pistol away. All the while the three-headed dog stood and watched her struggles dispassionately.

Finally, exhausted by the vigorous play and fearing she smelled entirely of dog, Faedra gave up on regaining her feet and struck the porch floor in frustration.

"If something as impossible as yourself is here, then surely

Elle's in trouble!" she said to the three-headed dog. "Why won't you do something?"

The three-headed dog simply stood like stone and stared at her.

"Elle!" she called loudly as the dogs head-butted her. "*Elle!* Come out, because I'm having a devil of a time trying to get to you!"

Tremors shook the house. She heard the windows rattle.

"*Elle!*" Faedra cried in fear.

The three-headed dog suddenly ran off the porch.

Faedra watched as it loped in a circle on the drive and drove its powerful body back to the porch. It jumped the railing. She ducked as the beast crashed through the bay window.

Faedra leapt to her feet to follow. The remaining dogs blocked her.

"Let me through!" she cried above their barking din.

They ignored her protestations and pushed her back.

"Beasts!" Faedra said in frustration as she stumbled off the porch.

She gasped when she saw Josefina and a young man through the plate glass of the doors. They pulled at the doors as if they were fighting the push of a great wind. The young man wedged his body into the opening they forced apart, and Josefina squeezed through.

But as Faedra bound up the stairs to get in, Josefina yanked the young man out and the doors slammed shut again. A dog grabbed Faedra's skirt with its mouth and pulled. She stumbled back down the steps.

"Oh!" she said, shaking her fist.

"Mrs Black is still inside!" Josefina cried to her.

The dog abruptly let Faedra go. She ran for the doors and rattled the handles. The dogs jumped and scratched at the glass panes.

"Now they're locked!" she exclaimed.

She heard a great explosion within that shook everything.

In the reception area with the belching pit, Elle picked up a piece of floor tile and approached a gaslight. She no longer heard the three-headed dog. She smashed the gaslight's crystal globe, dropped the tile, and pulled out the remaining dynamite sticks from her waistband. She began lighting them in the gas flame.

"This is for Neville Lunt and Eden Brunch," she called out. She tossed the stick towards the flashing pit.

"This is for Fidela Sweetwater and Mr Hardwick," she said, tossing the second lit stick.

"And this one," she said as the third stick's fuse flared. "Is for Hekate's great dog. But most of all, Abigail, this one is for *me*." Elle threw the third stick down the pit. She turned and ran as fast as she could for the hallway.

She saw Austin wedged between the entry doors, but before she could call, he pulled through. The doors shut with a loud slam. Black dogs jumped before the doors. Elle saw Faedra through the plated glass and her heart leapt.

The explosion deafened her. Debris whistled by and she saw the dust cloud roll past her. The floors and walls shook as she fought to keep her feet and move forwards. Faedra fiddled with the doors and then stepped back, pointing her silver Smith & Wesson. Elle watched her turn her head away and fire into the lock.

Oh darling! Elle thought, faintly hearing the gunshot. *You told me yourself that shooting locks only works in penny drea—*

She watched Faedra, Austin, Josefina, and the black dogs push hard against the doors and force them open again.

Lucky us! Elle thought. She then realised that for all her running, she still hadn't reached the entrance. The hallway was twisting; gaslights disappeared and became lit candle fixtures. The colours of the wallpaper changed. Elle ran even as her floor slowly rotated to become a wall and her ceiling twisted to become the floor. She felt she was nearly running upside-down.

Her step slowed in the phantom reality enveloping her. She moved as if in syrup and heard a woman laugh madly, the sound surrounding her.

I've a wife to go to, Abigail, Elle thought as wood panels splintered nearby. *So dwell on that, you noxious bitch!*

She marshalled all her power and imagined it an impenetrable second skin around her. Her feet lifted into the air. The shaking floor fell to pieces.

Elle flew. She pushed her body towards the flung-open doors. The walls rattled apart around her. Even as she focused upon Faedra's outstretched hand, she saw a place of darkness from the corner of her eye. Within that dark stood a staring woman with three faces, the forward visage dispassionately observing her as she passed. Elle thought her nude, though her brow wore stars and in four separate hands she carried objects: flaming twin torches, a key, a long dagger, and a scourge. One of her faces was of a black dog. Her hand with the torches pointed to the doors.

Elle reached for the doors. She felt Faedra, Josefina, and Austin lay hands upon her. They hauled her through the collapsing entrance just as her vision shadowed and all fell to black.

CHAPTER TEN

When Elle woke, it was without opening her eyes. Her head was a great and tender weight, filled with delicate pain. She knew she lay in a bed; she felt the pillow beneath her head and the blankets covering her. Her arms lay atop. She moved her hand.

She felt someone take it in a warm, comforting grasp and determined right away that it was Faedra, for a second hand gently touched her cheek. Elle worked her throat and found it dry.

Faedra removed her hands and Elle heard a water glass clink. Then she felt it at her lips. She managed a few sips.

"Is the house dead?" Elle feebly said.

"It is," Faedra answered. Her hand returned to Elle's cheek.

"Are . . . Austin and Josefina safe?"

"They are."

Elle frowned, still unable to open her eyes.

"Am I under arrest?" she said.

"No, dear. But we are still in Chiselhurst, in the Bromley Town

Hotel, at the request of the police."

"Make them . . . pay for our room."

"I will."

Elle turned her head and pressed her lips to Faedra's warm, bare hand.

She fell asleep.

Elle woke again in the afternoon and managed to pry her eyes open. Head still delicate, she felt less the pounded-flat person she had been hours before. The sticking plaster on her forehead was not so very big, and Faedra assured her the wound was but a surface gash from cutting herself on the constable's badge. The constable, she was happy to learn, woke despite his own head wound and would survive to police another day. She herself had been unconscious since the events of yesterday.

"Only yesterday? Oh, that is an improvement, far better than when I was bedridden for three days!" Elle said, as Faedra helped her in and out of bed for the water closet. "Perhaps my brain's tolerance for my esemplastic powers is improving. But we can't afford this impromptu holiday! What of your position, dear? Don't your tenants need you?"

"Don't give them a thought. Only concentrate on your rapid regaining of health," Faedra said cheerfully.

"You are proper motivation for my return to vigour," Elle whispered to her, and Faedra smiled broadly.

Elle was coaxing Faedra to climb into bed with her when there was a knock at the door. After Faedra straightened her clothes and Elle was back in bed and wrapped in her dressing gown, they bade the person enter. A tall, blond clean-shaven fellow looked in. His blue eyes were friendly and his manner cheerful. Elle liked his smile.

"I'm Sgt Barkley, Mrs Black," he said as he walked in. In his hands he carried a stool. He had a light-hearted step. He turned to wave in a dark-haired woman wearing spectacles. When she entered, Elle saw she had a folding typewriter's case in one hand and a collapsible table in the other.

"And this is Miss Temple, the typist. We'll try not to remain too long and disturb your rest further. But you've had quite the adventure! I only need your story of what happened at the Sundark."

"And especially of the last day?" Elle said. "I'm sorry for the lost policemen."

"Men lost like that is why we've a Secret Commission! So they can handle matters like these, a man-eating house! But we didn't know it ate people until you came to investigate, Mrs Black. I've the notes taken by the inspectors who formerly had this case, but as those fellows expired before completing them, I'd like to hear what you have to say."

Elle acquiesced, and Sgt Barkley found a chair while Miss Temple situated herself on her stool and set up her typewriter. Faedra sat on the bed beside Elle and held her hand. At the sergeant's prompting, Elle unfolded the story of her experiences at the Sundark while Miss Temple typed.

Elle's evening meal arrived when she'd finished with what the sergeant wished to hear. Barkley thanked her, and Miss Temple took that as her sign to pack her typewriter and leave. But when Josefina and Austin appeared at the doorway, eager to see how Elle was doing, Barkley managed to dawdle. He faded into the background and took a seat at the windowsill as her relieved friends entered. He went over the notes in his notebook. Elle thought his ability to seem invisible an interesting technique for so seemingly cheerful and talkative a man.

After expressing thankfulness that she was well, Josefina and Austin encouraged her to proceed with her meal, which Elle thought very impolite of her to do. But she was very hungry and Faedra had ordered her a beefsteak. It was an obscenely extravagant expense and therefore could not be wasted. Even as she ate heartily, she noted Josefina's drawn look and that she wore a black ribbon, pinned to her bodice.

"Mrs Black, I think I might try writing a story for *The Strand* of our Sundark experiences," Austin said. "Illustrated with my photographs, of course. But . . . I do wonder about certain things. Were you always of the mind that it was Abigail Sundark's essence that possessed the house, and not Alana Hardwick's?"

"I keep as open a mind as possible, Mr Washington. No-one is above suspicion. But to answer your question, it was the apparitions. They were always of Abigail's story, from her point of view. If Alana's essence were in possession of the house, the phenomena should have reflected upon her life."

"If Mrs Hardwick did not . . . appear in the garden, Mrs Black," Josefina said. "Where she be?"

"I think she's inside the house still," Elle said. "Or what's left of her. Hidden by her murderess. In that regard, Mr Hardwick's insistence that Alana was still there and not fled or taken elsewhere had always been correct.

"Abigail Sundark knew that by taking Alana away so completely and mysteriously Mr Hardwick could only stay, left to helplessly wonder and obsess for some answer, even one he may fear. The other guests she simply murdered, strengthened by their sacrificed essences, and spat out their remains."

Elle quickly ate the last of her steak before she could recall ghastly details like Neville Lunt's severed hand.

"Her house guests, from when she was alive and living in the Sundark," Austin said thoughtfully. "She was murdering even then?"

"Yes," Elle said. "I believe she fed Sundark like one would a pet. Or . . . a trapped goddess. Though I wonder about Minona Hodges, Heric's ward and assistant. I fear that like Alana, she wasn't simply murdered. Abigail probably imprisoned the poor child deep inside."

"It sounds like jealousy," Faedra said.

"You've deduced it, dear. Abigail felt as threatened by her husband's fondness for the girl as she did by Mr Hardwick's for Miss Dufish. Perhaps when Minona disappeared, Heric had enough and removed himself from his wife forever."

"But," Austin said as Josefina stared at Elle. "But the house never . . . I mean unless it had tried to? Take Miss Dufish, I mean."

"I can only surmise, Mr Washington, that Abigail was aware that ridding herself of Miss Dufish might give Mr Hardwick the reason to finally give up his mad quest. With Miss Dufish's continued assistance in managing the house, Mr Hardwick was free to prolong his futile search. Though I believe that Abigail became upset when Miss Dufish returned from her trip to Camden Town. Perhaps she'd thought Josefina had fled. Thus, the shattering of the drawing room's mirror."

Elle turned to Josefina.

"All that time Mr Hardwick spent on the engines, mapping them, taking them apart, he was really looking for Alana," Elle said gently. "And each night that he gazed up from the Sidereal Dome, he hoped to catch a glimpse of her, feel her, be gifted some preternatural sign by her. And perhaps he also went, every night, to give her the opportunity to finally abduct him into the sky and join her."

Austin made a sound, half laughter and half scorn, and shook his head.

"What you describe was how he was," Josefina said quietly.

Elle wiped her mouth with her napkin, her meal done. The hotel's Apple Snow pudding, she thought, had been nearly as good as her own.

Austin then took the occasion to give out tintypes. He pulled them out of a pocket and handed Elle a card mounted tintype of herself, taken at the Sundark, and gave Josefina one of Mr Hardwick, standing sternly and in proper dress before the Sundark's drawing room overmantle.

"Oh! This is the photograph you took of me on the porch!" Elle turned to Faedra. "See here, dear! I'm knitting."

"I'd still like to photograph you whilst you demonstrate your powers, Mrs Black," Austin said.

Elle looked askance at him and Austin only smiled. He touched his hat.

Austin excused himself, pleading a desire to attend the cold supper buffet below before all the choicer dishes were gone.

Josefina remained, and the silent Barkley closed his notebook, touched his forehead with a smile, and slipped out the door. Faedra put the dinner tray on the table. Elle waited while Josefina ruminated. When Josefina finally looked at Elle, her gaze was questioning.

"Mr Hardwick be dead," she said.

"He is," Elle gently said.

Josefina's gaze searched Elle's for more answers.

"His sacrifice was meant to facilitate Abigail Sundark's self-destruction," Elle said. "And he might have been right. Without him, without any of us, there's no reason for that house to continue living."

Josefina looked at the tintype in her hand. She rose, her jaw resolute.

"I will bring *true* shamans here, Mrs Black. From America, Africa, Tibet. If Mr Hardwick and Alana be in the grip of that evil duppy still, in the Fourth Dimension, I be making certain that she goes to her eternal reward."

When Josefina left, there were two bank notes of twenty pounds each laid on the table for Elle's widows and orphans fund. Faedra solemnly folded them and tucked them in her bodice. Elle couldn't help but think of how the amount was half Faedra's yearly salary.

"That evil spirit is certainly deserving of her anger," Faedra said.

"She is more than angry at Abigail Sundark," Elle said. "She is angry with Mr Hardwick."

"She was in love with him, I believe," Faedra said softly.

"Yes. And just like a man, he left our Earth due to a wildly inflated sense of duty."

"Yet Mr Hardwick's decision was commendable, wasn't it? I . . . I might have done the same." Faedra sat by Elle.

"Oh Faedy." Elle took hold of her and held tightly. "It was.

Just never fight in a duel, dear. Oh please. Someone is always left behind."

Elle, to her chagrin, slept through most of the next morning and therefore they could not depart their hotel until long after midday. Bags packed and Elle hoping her sticking plaster wasn't too ghastly a sight, they avoided the journalists who laid in wait in the lobby by exiting in back. They boarded their carriage for Camden Town.

Elle fretted about the possible state of their villa home in her absence. She worried aloud if Faedra would still love her despite the horrible scar her forehead was sure to bear. She clucked at remembering the bloodstains drying on her packed dress.

"It must be soaked in salted water," she said.

"You are such a silly goose," Faedra said, but her wide smile of amusement was just reward for Elle's frivolous ramblings.

They heard a hail from someone running outside and then a rap on the carriage door. Their vehicle came to a stop. Austin opened the door, greeted them, and they invited him in.

He climbed in with his camera mounted on its tripod. Taking the seat opposite Elle and Faedra, he grinned. Elle had never seen him happier. The carriage resumed its journey.

"Mr Washington, as much as I enjoy your company, I've tolerated your impropriety long enough," Elle said in good humour. "I prefer that you remove your hat before my wife."

Austin sheepishly looked down. He put a hand to his hat and slowly removed it. His hair was blond and with the wavy curls of African men. He ran a hand over them.

"Your hair is beautiful, Mr Washington," Elle said.

"Thank you, Mrs Black," he quietly said. "I've been a long time trying to pass as one of your race. Miss Dufish guessed right away, of course. My mother is white, my black father was . . . well, that's still a hard story to share. He was murdered, you see, hung and set afire for being who he was, and the ones who did it made a picnic affair of his killing. And perhaps I chase apparitions wondering if I'll ever have the courage to go back to that place of his death and find him."

"We're sorry," Faedra said softly.

"The violence of his death has long complicated my life," Austin said. "But today, perhaps its effects are less. Unlike Mr Hardwick, I can see opportunities beyond what haunts me. I'd be a fool not to try for happiness. You both have helped me understand. We *are* living in a different society, aren't we, Mrs White-Black?"

Faedra smiled broadly. "We are in England, Mr Washington."

He nodded, his smile matching hers. He turned to Elle. "I only wanted to thank you for all you've done. Now, I admit, I didn't know what to make of your marriage when you first spoke of it. But when we conversed that day in the reception area, I realised I didn't want to think any longer like one who stood in judgement of another. We would not be alive if it weren't for you. I've still an ambition to pursue with the Society of Psychical Research, but if need be, that can wait so that I can give my most sincere attentions to another."

He played with the brim of his hat in embarrassment. Elle reached and patted his hand.

"Just make certain your mother sends you more wonderful food items from America," she said. "Miss Dufish finds great happiness in preparing them."

Their carriage reached the gates of Sundark. Faedra bade the driver halt so Austin could disembark. He intended to take more photographs to document the Sundark, its garden, and the barn. As he departed, making his laborious way up the drive, Elle looked up the hill.

The house was a pile of burnt wood and rubble, glittering with shattered art glass. Dark plumes of smoke rose from the wreckage. A fire carriage stood nearby, the horse munching contentedly on grass. The lone fireman idly sprayed a slow arc of water from his hip like a man urinating.

"No sign of the dogs. Ah well. I'm sure they're well," Faedra said. "It's been nearly two days, yet a fire still burns from its depths."

"It is fuelled by hell," Elle said.

Alarmed, Faedra looked at her as the carriage started again.

"I jest," Elle said. A fresh breeze entered the window, chasing the scent of smoke away. "It is only the boilers. If any try to repair and salvage them, they may experience a surprise. For surely it would be the place the last of Abigail Sundark may try to reside in."

"I don't understand. You told Miss Dufish that Mr Hardwick's sacrifice would see to Abigail's end."

"I only said thus so that Josefina's last thought of him needn't be that he had made yet another futile attempt to seek Alana." Elle sighed. "He saw an opportunity to leave our plane for another and leapt for it. Abigail took his essence. I can't know what that truly means. And I still can't say how Abigail Sundark became married to the house in the manner we found her, stored in that mechanical coffin. Of whether she put herself there or if her husband did."

"You mean . . . she might have been murdered in turn?" Faedra said in a hushed voice.

Elle recalled the apparitions of Heric she'd seen.

"It is a thought. In the end, her true mate was the house. Whether she was murdered or went to her fate intentionally, her symbiotic existence was a form of eternal living, wasn't it? It was knowledge stolen and harnessed of a chthonic being, a mechanical ensorcellment that would have Abigail and her victims exist forever, betwixt and between. Had we, her inmates, all died and disappeared, she need only sleep until more came to live at the Sundark."

"Elle," Faedra said in concern.

"I am no exorcist!" Elle said. "Don't worry, dear, I will write Miss Dufish straightaway about Abigail's bowels."

"Cheeky kit," Faedra said with a smile. "But I do admire Miss Dufish's determination. It stirred me to hear her speak of giving that evil spirit its due! How unburdened our hearts would be, knowing unfinished matters can be taken care of in so decisive a manner. I am happy that Mr Washington, too, has found a measure of conclusion with his father's poor ghost."

Elle did not answer, her hand on Faedra's knee. She thought about her apparition of Valentin.

They reached home as afternoon turned to evening, and Elle was delighted to see her two sphinxes. She showered them with praise and attention. She inspected the downstairs, her garden, and the kitchen while Faedra carried their cases and carpetbag upstairs. Elle found that Mrs Haggins had thoughtfully prepared a cold meal of meats, bread, pudding, and a jelly mould, placed beneath covers, with a note to welcome her home. Elle ascended to join Faedra in the bedroom.

Faedra, busy with unpacking all of Elle's things, expressed concern at the broken chatelaine, took stock of Elle's remaining candles and empty self-heating cans, and thought aloud of how she might improve Elle's detecting equipage. Elle turned her around, kissed her, undressed her, and then undressed herself.

In her eagerness to clear the bed of her luggage's contents, she dumped the coverlet on the floor.

It was very late at night when Elle woke suddenly, disturbed by something that she knew was not a sound, merely a feeling. Faedra slept deeply beside her.

Elle sat up. There was someone outside, on the tiny balcony of the bedroom. The intruder made no sound. She rose and donned her dressing gown. As she stepped quietly across the room on bare feet she saw the outline of a figure through the gauzy curtains of the balcony doors. The moonlight gave the figure a shadow.

She stopped when she saw the balcony doors slowly open.

The curtains blew. A man stepped forwards, tall and dark-haired. He wore the black evening clothes of a gentleman.

Elle stared at his calm profile and cut cheekbones as he slowly looked about the room. His eyes were heavy-lidded and slightly slanted, feline-like.

Before his gaze reached her, she stepped closer and faced Valentin. She laid her hands on him.

He started at her touch and she was surprised to feel his reaction. He then relaxed, his searching gaze deep with unfathomable emotions that she did not want to acknowledge. She pushed him, finding him solid and unyielding.

For some reason, that angered her. With trembling hands, she quickly unbuttoned his silk waistcoat and pushed his white tie aside. She gripped his white shirt and with a hard tug, pulled it apart. His shirt buttons popped off and pitter-pattered on the carpeting.

She saw his chest, as well formed and muscled as she had remembered. She ran her fingers through his chest hairs, searching. She kept looking and heard him chuckle.

"Such a dream!" she murmured. "That I can touch you, so! And you, still smelling so sweet." She ceased her search and put her hands to her face.

"No wound," she said, her voice rising. "No coin. You haven't even the decency to be as I remembered."

"Elle," Valentin said.

"Why come to me perfect?"

"Elle . . ."

"Well, if you must talk, what is it?" she said.

He raised an eyebrow.

"How different you are now," he said softly. "More 'woman' than I knew."

"Because I'm no longer a child?"

"Yes. But you've not yet the swells of a mother."

"That's too much observation for a ghost," she said.

She saw Valentin's gaze search her face.

"Concern? Really?" she said. She laughed. "Too late for that."

"Did you bury me, Elle?" he whispered.

"Of course I did," she said in a hushed voice. "I could not stand by your grave. I was on my knees, muddied and dying in heart and mind when they lowered your coffin into the ground."

"Were you to dig that coffin up, you would not find me in it," he gently said.

"Did you do what Hector accused you of? Was it you who took everything?" Elle asked.

Valentin's chin dropped to his chest and he looked at her.

"I did," he said.

She stared into his eyes, thinking him unchanged and perfectly as he had been, five years before. His wavy hair cut the same, his moustache trimmed just so. His beautiful eyelashes.

"You are not an apparition," Elle said. "Your eyes are living. You feel like one who is *truly* here, betwixt and between! But . . . I can create such a vision, especially while deeply sleeping. Therefore, you dream-thing, you . . . manifestation of a need! Though I've asked my question somehow you are still here. What foolish desire do I have that still wants answer?"

"I am not lost, Elle," Valentin said. "I am truly here. Touch this."

He took hold of her left hand and raised it to his face. He bared his teeth.

She saw fangs and her fingers stiffened. He touched her rigid forefinger to the sharp tip of one canine.

"Look at me, Elle," he said.

Elle looked up. She fell into his gaze, his irises glittering with secrets.

She snatched back her hand and felt the side of her neck. Beneath her fingers she felt the twin scars she had never been able to explain to Faedra.

"Yes. You remember now. Only because I've let the memory return to you," Valentin said. "We are capable of beguilement. But be assured, I only bit you once."

"It hurt," she whispered.

Valentin smiled. She thought it self-deprecating, despite the sharp teeth.

"A necessary part of what I am," he said.

She shoved him.

"Elle," he said in surprise.

"Go," she said.

"Do you really want me to?" Valentin asked.

"Once, I loved you," Elle said. "And never mind that now I know that you are some . . . and stole from me! I loved you but it was an inadequate love. I question now whether I'd ever inspired a deep and consuming passion within you. Did you playact for me, Valentin? Was our marriage a lark for you to perform your part?"

She watched as Valentin's face grew solemn.

"You were a beautiful companion," she said. "My friend, my confidante. How I loved you. But that would not have been enough to keep us happy. And how do I know this? Because this time, I've a true love, one I don't doubt would come for me even if I lay beyond. I simply love her. All of her. She is everything."

Valentin stared, his visage devoid of emotion, and Elle realised what the familiar enigmatic look meant that had so infuriated her years ago. Her former husband was perplexed.

A smile curled his lips and his eyes twinkled.

"Then perhaps you do not need my apology," he said.

"I will take it," she said.

"And take what I will offer, for it was my intention in seeking you out tonight. Especially after . . . seeing you again. I've read of this Sundark adventure. I do not like it that you put yourself in danger. If ever you need it, call upon my help, Elle."

"I won't be needing it. Go now, Valentin."

He held out his hand.

Elle chastised herself even as her own hand rose to respond to the polite gesture. Valentin gently accepted her fingers and kissed them. His lips pressed softly against her skin, his eyes closed. Elle remembered the feel of his mouth in intimate places. When he released her hand, he grinned mischievously.

"Your wife is beautiful," he said.

He stepped back. The balcony doors abruptly shut. Elle quickly parted the curtains. Even as she stared through the glass at the moonlit night, she could not see him outside, anywhere. She turned, thinking of Faedra.

She saw Faedra standing with arm raised, aiming her Smith & Wesson at where Valentin had been. She wore no clothes.

"Faedra! *He saw you?*" Elle cried.

Faedra slowly lowered her arm and looked down at her state of undress.

"Well, I was in a hurry, Elle! I only had time to fetch my pistol," Faedra said.

"Such a sight you've given him! Now he'll surely return!" Elle said. "Oh Faedra, he's an utter rake!"

"So that was Valentin," Faedra said pensively.

"Why did you not speak?" Elle demanded.

"Darling, you were doing quite well by yourself and needed this time with him. He knew all the while I would shoot. After I pulled you out of harm's way first," Faedra said. "Now I wonder if my weapon would have done any good."

"Oh!" Elle said. She stamped her foot. "Will you get back in bed, this instant! How fortunate for you that I'm not the sort who disciplines!"

"It's I who should discipline you," Faedra retorted. "The way you ran your fingers on his curly chest. You did not look down and therefore witness the prominent evidence of his pleasure."

"Really, Faedy? And you blame my touch? When you are the one standing there as God made you? I should mete out that spanking!"

"How you promise," Faedra said.

She tossed her head and walked back to the bed, deliberately swaying her bare derriere.

Once Faedra put her pistol away, Elle ran to her and smothered her with kisses. They tipped into the bed. Elle shrugged out of her dressing gown and knelt over Faedra. Her hair cascaded down and Faedra smoothed it away.

"This is not a dream," Elle said.

"It is not, darling," Faedra said.

"I love you love you love you," Elle said.

She kissed Faedra more, but Faedra took a moment to catch her breath.

"He's a creature, Elle! And now you know, he's also a scoundrel. I wonder if he really came tonight to apologise," Faedra said.

"He is of no concern to us," Elle said, bending to kiss Faedra's chest.

"And when he was your husband, you never saw those fangs?" Faedra said.

"I was nineteen, Faedy, and deeply beguiled."

"He might be watching," Faedra said breathlessly.

"Good," Elle said. She moved lower.

At dawn, Lt Montague's rooster crowed. Elle rose, Faedra still fast asleep, and went to the balcony doors. She picked up the silver-plated shirt buttons dotting the floor.

On the front of the buttons was a floral design. She turned one over and read the back:

Solidaire, AP&C Paris

She thought of the gold-gilt buttons she had carefully picked and sewn on an embroidered shirt that had been her wedding gift to him. She closed her fist around the buttons.

"Real," she whispered. "And a vampyre."

When Faedra finally woke, Elle had already bathed and dressed, opened all the drapes, cleaned the lamps, cooked breakfast, and sealed four jars of strawberry preserves while Mrs Haggins used the hot water spigot of the bedroom's stove to fill buckets for Faedra's bath. Elle cooked more as Faedra bathed and dressed. She packed her a tidy midday meal of butter-fried trout, mashed potatoes, parboiled sea kale, strawberries, and crusty bread in a petite, sectioned hay box wrapped in a flower-patterned, cotton drawstring bag.

Usually, Faedra would frequent the luncheon rooms, especially to meet a colleague or Elle herself, who joined her spouse once a week within greater London while volunteering at the soup kitchen. But in the interest of frugality, Elle insisted on providing Faedra with a portable meal at least a few days of the week, which her spouse ate with coffee and a soup ordered at a coffeehouse.

Faedra descended for breakfast, and they sat down to boiled eggs, smoked haddock, new potatoes, deviled kidneys, toast, bacon, fried tomatoes, and blood sausage. During the meal, Elle handed Faedra her coin purse, replenished with Faedra's weekly allowance.

"You may treat yourself to whelks, dear," Elle said.

"Oh, darling, thank you!" Faedra said. "Now I hadn't spent hardly at all when you were gone, just on coffee and the omnibus fare."

"I noticed," Elle said, smiling. "And before then, you bought me chocolates. But you did come to rescue me while I was in a dreadful state and paid for the hotel room when the police refused to. You deserve your street foods."

"I will have just a few periwinkles. But won't you like some too?" Faedra said.

"Bring them back in your hay box and I will have them," Elle said.

When she kissed Faedra farewell at the door, Elle thought her wife left in cheery spirits.

She searched through her parents' books on gods and goddesses of antiquity, then departed for Bloomsbury Market in Bury Place, basket in hand and wearing her plum-coloured dress and matching bonnet. On the omnibus she knitted. At market, she found a spice merchant who sold frankincense and a flower seller who provided fresh asphodel flowers. She bought a box of choice, sweet cakes.

As she wandered around butcher stalls and dallied over costermonger barrows loaded with fish and vegetables, she thought of Faedra in her noisy city surroundings, partaking of the rough food from street vendors, knocking on strange doors to investigate tenants, and having vigorous discussions with workwomen. She caught another omnibus and rode it back to Camden Town.

Elle walked home. She entered Lt Montague's garden, the

hens clucking around her feet, and laid her purchases down on the low garden wall they shared. Then she retrieved her egg box stored near his scullery door. She picked fresh eggs from his chicken coop. Elle departed Lt Montague's gate and entered her own garden just as Mrs Haggins picked up the purchases sat on the wall.

"Oh, Mrs Black, asphodels?" Mrs Haggins said worriedly. "In whose remembrance are these for?"

"Mrs Haggins, people had lost their lives at the Sundark, but these flowers are for something else, entirely."

"The Sundark affair!" Mrs Haggins exclaimed. "Oh, what a stir it has created! It's all I can do to keep myself from taking a broom to these nagging journalists!"

"Mrs Haggins, what do you mean?" Elle said. They both returned inside. She arranged all her purchases on the kitchen table, separating out those she would offer to the goddess Hekate: the frankincense, asphodel flowers, and cakes. She would add the best strawberries from her hotbed to the offering.

"Well, I've been telling the journalists who came knocking that you were out for the day, ma'am," Mrs Haggins said. "But they persisted in wanting entry, even at the back gate! I made certain they were gone before you returned but there is one lingering still, in front."

"Mrs Haggins, I am grateful for your vigilance!" Elle said. "Faedy will not like it if I should become well-known. Nor will I. I'll see to this fellow at the front."

"Ma'am, it's not a man but a woman, and a very odd one! I've been wary of speaking to her and was hoping she'd tire and go away," Mrs Haggins said.

"Odd?" Elle said, smiling. "Then I must see."

After asking Mrs Haggins to put a jar of strawberry preserves in Lt Montague's kitchen, Elle went to her front door and opened it. The first thing she saw was a very large penny-farthing with a treadle pedal, resting against their home's low iron fence. Then, as she looked down, she spied a woman's brown cavalier hat with owl feathers, perched on the head of a crouching woman in discussion with the twin sphinx statues. The woman wore a leather half-mask.

"Now I understand that you must ask a riddle, but what if I offered you a story instead?" the masked woman said to the sphinxes in a low voice. "Then, if you don't enjoy it, you may eat me! But I know you'll enjoy it. Once upon a time there was a woman in love with a woman, and when the second woman died, the first had her love resurrected—"

"May I listen to the story too?" Elle asked.

The woman rose, smiling. Her blue eyes sparkled as she took in Elle's eyes and hair.

"Oh my! But what do I see? Night-wandering daughter, 'she who stands protected by two rampant lions'!" she exclaimed.

Elle started in dismay.

"You mustn't say that," Elle cautioned. "Oh, never! You are speaking of Hekate, and I'm certainly not that."

The woman's smile was mirthful, and Elle was taken by this stranger's ease with discussing chthonic beings.

"I believe you were sharing a story?" Elle demanded with an eyebrow raised.

"Oh, but it's meant to be a secret," the woman said. "For a sphinx holds many such secrets."

Elle smiled. "She does. They both do. Now, I was in the midst of something quite important, so may I enquire as to your business?"

"Mrs Black, I presume?" The woman smiled genially. "I am Helia Skycourt. How do you do?"

"How do you do," Elle said offering her hand.

"Forgive my presence, Mrs Black." Helia accepted her hand with a warm squeeze. After releasing it she presented Elle with a card. "For I've heard of your recent encounter with the Sundark Hotel and hope you might tell me more, as I specialise in supernatural matters. I am a journalist for *The Times*."

While Elle read the silver-engraved card, Helia leaned forwards.

"The sphinx told me you once were in an asylum, Mrs Black," Helia said in a low voice. "I was in one too."

Elle looked into Helia's twinkling eyes and saw mischief

in them.

Elle giggled behind her hand. Helia giggled with her.

"And I've heard of you, Miss Skycourt," Elle said, smiling. "Very well. I'll grant you an interview. But you must do me a favour in return."

"Gladly. And what is that?"

"Help me make an offering to a chthonic deity, for I've never done such a thing before. Then, you must tell me what you know of vampyres. Come in."

The end.

Character Key

(in order of appearance):

Mrs Elle (Eleanor) Black (formerly Mrs Valentin Black, née Dunny).
Mrs Faedra White-Black (wife to Elle)
Valentin Black (Elle's dead husband)
Mrs Haggins (the Mrs Blacks' housekeeper)
Royal Navy Lieutenant Elmer Montague (neighbour to the Mrs Blacks)
Miss Josefina Dufish (secretary to Mr Hardwick)
Mr Arch (Sundark driver)
Mr and Mrs Willy (staff at Sundark)
Mr Neville Lunt (tin salesman)
Mr Austin Washington (ghost chaser)
Miss Eden Brunch, Miss Fidela Sweetwater (spiritualists)
Mr Hardwick (present owner of Sundark)
Heric Sundark (illusionist and designer of Sundark)
Abigail Sundark (occultist wife to Heric)
Mrs Hemrold Speckings (wife to the engineer who helped build Sundark)
Miss Minona Hodges (assistant to Heric)
Alana Hardwick (wife to Mr Hardwick)
Sgt Barkley (investigating plainclothes policeman)
Miss Temple (typist for hire)

Author Notes

Miss Eden Brunch's invocation to Hekate:
I used the true names and titles as given for Hekate and all six of the *Voces Magicae*. Seeing as these were authentic Words of Power from antiquity, I decided to resort to the old-time remedy for "words or situations too sensitive to bear or share": the dashes. Yes, I am the superstitious sort.

To write all the particulars about Hekate and her circumstances in this story, I consulted the following material:

Hekate Liminal Rites: A Historical Study of the Magic, Spells, Rituals and Symbols of the Torch-Bearing Triple Goddess of the Crossroads, by David Rankine and Sorita D'Este, published by Avalonia (May 24, 2009), ISBN 978-1905297238.

Hymn VI: To Hekate and Janus
By Proclus Diadochus (410-485 AD)
(Text: E. Vogt Procli Hymni Weisbaden 1957)
As excerpted from: The Goddess Hekate: Studies in Ancient Pagan and Christian Religion & Philosophy Volume I., Edited by Stephen Ronan. Chthonios Books. Hastings, UK. 1992
http://www.whiterosesgarden.com/book_of_shadows/other_books/historical_BOS/hymns_to_hekate.htm

Book Five of Praeparatio Evangelica, by Eusebius of Caesarea.
http://www.tertullian.org/fathers/eusebius_pe_05_book5.htm

Ovid's Metamorphoses, Book 7 (Medea and Jason, part 179), translation by Brookes Moore.
http://www.theoi.com/Text/OvidMetamorphoses7.html

For spirit paths:

Fairy Paths & Spirit Roads: Exploring Otherworldly Routes in the Old and New Worlds, by Paul Devereux, 2003, Chrysalis Books.

And for the Western historical tradition of female marriage from 1850-1890, before the term 'homosexuality' or 'lesbian' was invented:

Between Women: Friendship, Desire, and Marriage in Victorian England, by Sharon Marcus, 2007, Princeton University Press.

Illustrations

by
Elizabeth Watasin

When she was seated, she read the letter aloud.

She saw a woman move in the dark hall.

"Feel my thunderbolts!" she said.

"Hail! Hail! Hail! O night, night, night! Mighty Hekate of the Threshold!" she cried.

❖

A Glimpse Into:

Dark Victorian: BONES

"I Am Made of This"

Chapter One

A heavy fog rolled through London. Gaslights broke the dark as a hackney carriage drove down a deserted, cobbled street. Inside the carriage, Inspector Risk, a tall, dark-haired man with a thick moustache, sat and grimly regarded Dr. Speller, a bespectacled man with white mutton chop sideburns seated across from him. Dr. Speller moved his top hat around in his hands in excitement. The plainclothes sergeant, Barkley, took notes.

"It's Esther Stubbings, I'm sure of it," Dr. Speller said. "She is one of your victims."

"I've four bodies," Risk said. "Just skin and muscle. Full skeletons and organs entirely removed and no incisions made. Makes it hard to identify flattened faces. You're claiming that the organ almost sold to you tonight belonged to this Esther Stubbings, and therefore she's my victim."

"Well I've yet to identify the body, but the organ is

unquestionably hers, Inspector, because I was the surgeon," Speller said. "Every woman's reproductive organs are different. I mean in shape. I recognized my own work, sir; I was the one who removed her second ovary. And Esther was alive and well just last week. The only way someone could harvest her organs is if she were murdered."

"And since we've her female vitals she has been," Risk said. "So this organ stealer, knowing you were a women's physician and vivisectionist, he comes to you for a sale."

"I vivisected only to learn," Speller said. "But for the most part I now merely dissect organs purchased solely from the Royal Surgical Sciences Academy."

"Indeed. The Academy. Which buys from men like the one you met tonight," Risk said. "Except this one knows to bring it directly to you. The dead woman I have is of the poor. We know it from her clothes. How can someone like that afford your services?"

"She can when she volunteers for the procedure," Speller said. "Like all members of the Academy, I'm a man of science and medicine. Not only do I use the skills learned, I practice new techniques that have successfully corrected female ailments. Esther Stubbings was on her way to becoming a fully healthy woman. And none of it, thankfully, by use of supernatural nonsense, claiming healing through organ transference and such!"

"But that's exactly what I have, doctor," Risk said. "Black arts surgery. Unless you can explain how four people have no skulls, eyes, or brains in their intact heads Without them having been pulled out of their nostrils."

"Not to mention," Sergeant Barkley said, "how His Royal Highness can be here with us today if not for supernatural medicine. Been nineteen years since he nearly died! We've a bunch of nonsense to thank."

Risk sighed while Speller glowered. The carriage came to a halt outside a lit station house.

"You stay here," Risk said to Speller. "We'll move on to the mortuary shortly for you to identify the woman. And you," he said to Barkley. "Stop talking. Let's go."

When Risk stepped down from the carriage he saw a young woman in an azure coat briskly leave the station entrance. Her brown hat was crooked, and wisps of dark hair escaped. Her skirts were cut high enough for the ankles of her boots to show. She wore a fitted leather mask on one side of her face. Helia Skycourt smiled at Risk and waved. She grabbed the penny-farthing resting against the station wall, took a running jump into the sidesaddle seat, and hit the treadle. The lantern in front of her wheel suddenly lit. She sped away into the dark and fog.

Risk watched her depart, incredulous.

"Damn journalist," he said. "Does she never sleep?"

Barkley stifled a yawn. They entered the station building.

"Inspector," Barkley said in a low voice as they walked into the dimly lit room. A uniformed man was behind the desk. "This case . . . it being supernatural. When will the Secret Commission start helping?"

"When we ask for it," Risk said curtly. "And not before. What do you have?" he said to the policeman who rose to greet him.

"Sir," the policeman said. He led them down a narrow hall. "The fellow Dr. Speller had us arrest will be brought out of his cell shortly. He refuses to speak and has answered no questions. The doctor told us the man only spoke once during the negotiating of the price of the organ and his accent was German."

"Looks a foreigner, then?" Risk asked. He followed the policeman into a room with a desk and chairs. He took the seat behind the desk while Barkley went to stand near the small, barred window.

"No sir," the policeman answered. "Well dressed, clean-faced, trimmed hair, tidy, hands that haven't seen hard labor. I'm guessing he's of the medical profession."

"Organ stealers usually are," Risk said. "Especially those who work in mortuaries." They heard shuffling steps approach. Two policemen brought a shackled man into the room. He was a slim fellow, tight-lipped and with one, nervous eye. His other eye had been removed, leaving a gaping, black socket. He did not bother to shut his eyelid. The men escorting him sat him in front of Risk.

"*Wie ist dein name?*" Risk said.

The man looked at him in surprise.

"The sooner you answer our questions," Risk said. "The sooner we catch who's doing these black arts surgeries. Because it isn't you, is it? So if you don't want the blame, give us someone else's name."

The man's posture became stiffer.

"That's four dead," Risk said staring into the man's one eye. "Is the gallows worth this surgeon? Give him up and you won't have to worry. Do your sentence and then get on with life, right?"

Risk watched the man; the prisoner seemed to grow even more frightened.

"Right," Risk said slowly. "Now who is he?"

A shot exploded, shattering the window behind the sergeant. Blood sprayed into Risk's face. The other men shouted and ran out the door. The prisoner sat slumped. Brain matter hung from the side of his forehead where the bullet had exited.

Shouts and running came from outside the station. Risk didn't bother looking out the broken window, knowing that all he'd see would be darkness and fog. He grimly pulled out his handkerchief and slowly wiped his face. Barkley touched the prisoner to see if he was still alive.

"Shall I send a message to the Secret Commission?" Barkley asked.

Risk stared at the dead man who'd just brought him an internal affairs nightmare.

"Do it," he said.

❖

Read more in Elizabeth Watasin's
Dark Victorian: Bones

About The Author

Elizabeth Watasin is the acclaimed author of the Gothic steampunk series *The Dark Victorian* and the creator/artist of the indie comics series Charm School. She has worked as an animation artist on thirteen Disney feature films, including *Beauty and the Beast, Aladdin, The Lion King,* and *The Princess and the Frog,* and has written for *Disney Adventures* magazine. She lives in Los Angeles with her black cat named Draw, busy bringing readers uncanny heroines in shilling shockers and adventuress tales.
Follow the news of her latest projects at A-Girl Studio.
www.a-girlstudio.com
Visit her online at:
www.facebook.com/ElizabethWatasinX
twitter.com/ewatasin

Look for Elizabeth's third gothic tale in The Dark Victorian series:
EVERLIFE.
Then get ready for the second Elle Black Penny Dread: POISON GARDEN.

KEEP
CALM
GHOST
AND
SKULL
ARE
HERE